ROLO THE
PET EARTHLING

Hans Ness

Illustrated by
Sofia Komarenko
@narisofka

ZIRA PRESS • NEW BLORX

Copyright © 2023 Hans Ness
hansness.com

Illustrated by Sofia Komarenko
@narisofka

Zira Press
Pacifica, California
zirapress.com
Printed in the United States of America

1st edition 2023
Print master 11/10/23
Library of Congress Control Number: 2023907267
ISBN: 979-8-9880371-0-1

Contents

To Zorxablorg,
for such an unexpected journey.
Thanks for all the treats.

1. Zira's Wish

"Can't I have a pet earthling? Please?"

"Zira, we've been over this a dozen times. You're too young to handle such a big responsibility."

"But Mom, I promise I'll take real good care of it. I'll feed it every day, and take it on walks, and I'll give it baths."

Zira's mom pulled more groceries from the bag and leaned inside the refrigerator to cram the food on the shelves. "Earthlings are a lot of work, more than you think. And they make a big mess."

"But Mom—"

"Zira!" She withdrew her head from the refrigerator and finally looked at her. "I know you really want a pet, but we already have one."

"That's Lazro's pet!" moaned Zira. "And it just sits there and eats flies. It can't even talk!"

Her mom gave a forced smile. "Well, we can talk about this when you're older."

Zira had heard that line so many times before; it felt like a lie. She groaned and rolled her eyes as far as they could roll, then trudged back to her bedroom, loud enough for her mom to hear every frustrated footstep scuffing down the hallway. She tried slamming her door shut to punctuate her dramatic exit, but it got caught on a dirty sock on the carpet. She kicked the sock out of the way and shoved the door closed, not quite as loudly as she had hoped.

She belly-flopped onto her bed and buried her face in her pillow, wallowing in the blackness— exactly like the bleakness of her life, deprived of the fundamental right of having her own pet earthling. She lay there with her arms, legs, long black hair, and two antennae spread out in every direction, like a big green splat.

It was so unfair. She couldn't understand why her mom hated earthlings so much. She wasn't a little kid anymore, so why didn't her mom see how mature and responsible she was? Was this some punishment for something forgotten long ago? Or was she just mean for the sake of being mean? Parents just don't understand.

Perhaps she could find some way to be extra good to show her mom how responsible she was. Maybe she could do some extra chores around the house, or in the yard, or wash the car. Or maybe even clean her room. She looked around at all her clothes, toys, stuffed animals (mostly earthies, of course), books, art supplies, science kits, games, and gadgets—most of them lying on the floor, especially the dirty laundry. Ugh, that would be so much work.

She tried to think ... think ... but instead, her mind wandered to wondering what her pet earthling would be like. What type should she get? What kind of earthie would be so amazing it would make all her classmates jealous?

Perhaps her mom would let her have a different pet. Blorx is home to countless incredible creatures and critters of different hues, scales, furs, and forms, each with their own unique personalities and special talents.

Her big brother Lazro had a pet slurtle who could sing and imitate sounds. And he trained it to burp the alphabet. But most of the time, when not eating flies, it just tucked itself inside its blue spiral shell and did nothing.

A boundo likes to roll around its blabitrail tubes and tunnels, especially late at night when you're trying to sleep. If you have two boundos or more, they crash into each other and laugh hilariously with their squeaky little voices.

A kiffy may curl up in your lap and make a cute chortling sound if they like you. Or poke their claws into you if they don't. Or both—they're funny that way.

And a slipple can coil its fluffy, long, limbless body to hop like a spring. However, they do like to stare at you with their one giant eye, never blinking, even while they're asleep—which is a little creepy.

But Zira wanted a pet who could talk. There were only a few:

Squawklings understand everything you say. But they obey commands only if they're in the right mood. Maybe. And they can't actually talk so much as squawk word-like sounds. Really they think you should just speak *their* language.

Gruntlings can speak a little—basic words like yes, no, food, more, why, and toe. But usually they say nothing and judge you with their beady little eyes. And they might bite your toe if you offend them.

Blabblings can speak quite well—loquaciously with a splendiferous vocabulary—but they only want to talk about food, especially while still chewing it. And the only time they stop talking is when they're asleep.

Those were all adequate pets, Zira thought, good enough for other kids. But she had her heart set on an earthie. She liked how earthlings walk around on two legs and have two arms and two eyes, just like little blorxlings. They're very intelligent and can learn many tricks. And best of all, they can talk. Some even learn to read and write—even though they have no need to, and they cannot understand trans-dimensional verb tenses and quantum spelling. Zira knew five kids her age who already had pet earthlings. It was so unfair.

She decided her pet earthling would be a little young one while they're still so cute and soft— before they turn big, hairy, and lumpy. She thought maybe she would get a girl earthie with long black hair like hers, and they could wear matching outfits, and she'd name her Mira, like "mirror". Or Zirette. Or maybe a boy earthie with bright head-fur and speckles on his chubby cheeks, and she'd name him Figo. Or Brover. Or Gex. She wasn't sure yet.

But maybe this was all hopeless. After all, she had been begging her mom for *decades,* and the answer was always no.

...

If you have never been to Blorx before, you might be wondering what we blorxlings are like and how Zira could be so old. Let me explain.

Blorxlings are very much like you earthlings, and not at all like you at the same time. You might say we are like giants since we stand three times taller than you—but we are no monsters. Our faces are friendly, with large, shiny eyes and wide, gleaming smiles. Our skin is a bright green that glistens in the sunlight, and most of us have deep black hair. As you might expect, we have two antennae atop our heads that wiggle, point, and gesticulate our moods. And we age much slower than you and live about seven times longer. This is why a young girl like Zira was only seventy years old.

And obviously, we blorxlings are much, *much* smarter than you little earthlings. But I will admit: We are not always wiser.

2. Sulking

Lazro tapped on Zira's door and poked his head in.

"Hey Pea-Pod."

Zira was still lying on her bed, but now under a mound of all her plushy stuffed earthies, which she had piled on herself, with only her arms and legs sticking out.

"Hey Lazro," she said, muffled under the plushies.

He stepped into her room and sat on the edge of her bed. "What were you and Mom fighting about?"

She sighed dramatically and pushed the plushies off her face. "She still won't let me have an earthling."

"Oh, that."

"Why is she so mean?!" Zira whined.

"She's not mean—Well, sometimes. She just doesn't want the house all messy with pet toys or ... shedding or whatever. And that earthy smell. You know her."

"I'll clean up after it, and I'll vacuum. She won't even know!" Zira sighed again, spilling some of her stuffed toys onto the floor. "She still thinks I'm a little kid."

Lazro snickered.

Then a new strategy hatched in Zira's head. Her mom always liked Lazro best. "Will you talk to her for me?"

He shrugged. "I dunno what I'd say. It's hard to change her mind. Like you." He smiled.

"What if you say you'll help me bathe it and take care of it? She'd say yes to you ... She always does."

Lazro thought about this for a moment. "You know what?" He bopped her lightly on the face with a plushy. "I will."

...

That weekend on Blaturday morning, Zira was on the floor in her room, reading about the robot wars of 9812, when Lazro leaned through her doorway and said in a singsong voice, "Come on, Pea-Pod. We have a surprise for youuuu!"

He grinned at her, but it was an odd, goofy grin, not his normal, warm grin.

"What is it?" she asked.

"You'll see. Get your shoes on and get in the car."

"Where are we going?"

"So many questions!" he teased.

"But what's the surprise? Tell me!" Zira was never good at waiting.

He walked away down the hallway and hollered, "You'll see!"

Zira felt an explosion of excitement. She really didn't need to ask at all because she already had a good hunch. She slipped her shoes on and sprang to the garage, but no one was in the car yet. So she stepped back into the house and hollered, "Hurry up! Let's go!"

"One moment," their mom yelled from the kitchen.

Her big sister Riffa emerged from her bedroom. She was the middle child, closer to Lazro's age. "Yeah, Zira, hold your horfsies!" Riffa seemed to be in on the secret, too, because she was also giving Zira a weird smile.

Lazro hollered across the house, "Mom, where are the car keys?"

"Right where they alwa—"

"Never mind, found them!"

"Oh no," teased Riffa, "Lazro's driving?!"

Their mom shuffled toward the garage while organizing her purse. "Shush. He needs to practice for his license."

Riffa said to Lazro nasally, "Try not to hit any trash cans this time!"

"Ha ha," he sarcasticated.

They finally got in the car—a little too slowly, in Zira's opinion. She climbed in the back seat and wiggled with impatience. "C'mon! Let's go to the pet store!"

"The *pet store?*" said Lazro, overacting dramatically. "Who said anything about a *pet store?* No, Pea-Pod, we're taking you to the *dentist!*" He looked back at her with that goofy grin again.

3. Rolo's New Home

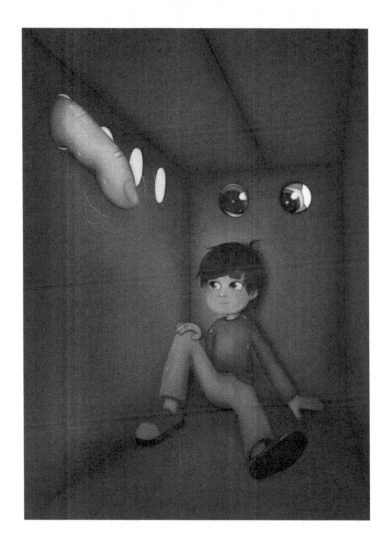

It was dark inside the cardboard box, with just a little ambient light shining from the twelve round air holes near the top. The young earthling boy tried to stand, but the box was too short. And besides, it was wobbling so much that he kept falling back down.

Zira cooed into the box with a sugary voice, "Are you ready to see your new home?"

The boy saw her large green eyes peering in, sliding from air hole to air hole. She poked her giant finger inside and waggled it about. He was too nervous to answer, but he was excited. He had just met Zira not long ago at the pet store, when she picked him out of all the other earthling kids in the pet pen. She had such a friendly face he already liked her, and he was eager to see his new home.

Finally, after much bumping, the box was still. Zira had set it on the family room carpet.

"Ready to come out now?" she asked sweetly.

He shifted his weight and prepared himself. "Okay, ready."

The two panels of the box roof opened upward. He squinted in the sudden brightness and tried to view the room. But before he could get oriented, Zira's giant hands reached toward him, scooped him out of the carrier box, and squeezed him against her chest.

"Here we are," she said cheerily, with an especially wide smile stretched across her face.

She plopped down on the carpet, and Riffa and Lazro kneeled close by. Riffa leaned even closer and cooed, "Hello there," as she reached out and ruffled his hair with her finger. "Can I hold him?"

Lazro said, "Let him get settled first."

All three of their giant heads were so close to the boy, staring with their giant eyes and breathing with their blorxling breath. He felt a bit intimidated.

Lazro suggested, "Why don't you let him walk around and explore?"

Their mom passed by at that moment, reorganizing her purse again. She stopped and nagged, "Make sure he doesn't pee on the carpet!"

"Mommm," groaned Zira, "he's already potty trained!"

"Don't worry, Mom," said Lazro. "I'll watch them."

She gave them a worried look, then, with a raised eyebrow and a shake of her head, she conceded and retreated from the room.

Zira gently set the boy down on the carpet.

He gazed in every direction. It was so different, he thought, not quite like what he had imagined a home would look like. And it smelled different, too, not like the pet store.

"Oh wait!" Zira jumped up, grabbed a shopping bag, and plopped down again so close to him that he was afraid she might crush him. "Look, here's your new toys!" She pulled out a bucket of squeaky balls, plastic dinovores, building blocks, and puzzles and poured them at his feet. Then she pulled out some clothes and held them up to him. "And here's a new outfit for you. And a blue one. And a green one." She tossed them on the floor. "And here's your brush." She rubbed it on his hair. "And this is your harness. And your leash. And your toothbrush." She tossed those too. "And here's your food bowl!"

He never had his own food bowl before.

Lazro asked, "What are you going to name him?"

"How about Bloogy?" suggested Riffa. "Or Mr. Frupples?"

Zira giggled.

The pet store had named him Durgur, which he did *not* like, so he was eager to get a new name.

Zira lifted him up and held him out with both hands to get a good look at him. Nervously, he estimated the distance to the floor so far below, but he trusted her. She peered at his little arms and legs, his little belly, his chubby cheeks and black head-fur, and his smiling brown eyes. "I'll name him ..." She thought carefully. "Rolo!"

He liked that. Rolo. It suited him.

...

Later, Zira, Riffa, and Lazro led Rolo on an expedition through all the rooms in their house. When it was dinner time, he got to try his new food in his new bowl. Then he got to try his new litter box. (Blorxian homes don't have pet-sized toilets.)

At the end of the night, Zira brushed his teeth, which he did *not* like. Then she tucked him into a little round pet bed in the corner of her room. He did not like that either.

"Can't I sleep in your bed?" he asked.

"I wish. But Mom was afraid I'd roll over on you, or you'd fall out or something. But I can see you here from my pillow. Okay, g'night." She kissed him on the head. "Don't let the earthworms bite."

"What?!" No one had warned him about the worms.

"Oh, never mind." She giggled. "That's just something we say. I don't know why. G'night."

Then she turned off the light and lay down in her bed.

Rolo tried to sleep, but he just rolled from side to side, onto his belly, and onto his back, over and over. An hour passed. It was too quiet. No yips, squeaks, or squeals from the other animals in the pet store—only a slight whistling noise from Zira's nose. And he wasn't huddled with other earthling kids sleeping in a pile. He felt lonely for the first time. So he got up and climbed the corner of her bed, then curled up against her warm chest. While still asleep, she wrapped her arm over him.

Rolo was home.

4. The Battle of Slime

"Commander Rolo, any sign of the enemy?" asked Zira, crouching behind the sofa.

"No, my empress," said Rolo, peering over the back of the sofa through toy binoculars way too big for him. "The coast is clear."

Several years had passed, and Rolo was now ten. But Zira, Riffa, and Lazro had barely grown, since earthlings grow up so much faster than blorxlings (or you might say blorxlings grow so much slower than earthlings).

"Let's move forward," she ordered. "Check the grand entry, Commander."

With his laser rifle in hand (bright green toy slime pistol), Rolo dashed out from behind the sofa and hid behind the corner of the grand entry (hallway). Zira commando-crawled behind him across the grass (carpet) with her sidearm (purple slime pistol). Rolo peered around the corner. No guards. He silently gave her several hand signals, badly imitating what he had seen in the movies. She signaled back, equally nonsensically, and they crept cautiously down the corridor.

Soon they reached the gates of the evil queen's throne room (Riffa's bedroom door).

"Check the gate," Zira ordered.

Rolo pushed, but it would not budge. "It's barricaded."

Zira reached up and released the drawbar (turned the doorknob). The gate swung open with an eerie creak. They slid inside.

"The Scepter of Doom has got to be in here," Zira whispered. "We must steal it and foil the sinister plan of the Evil Queen Rifaffa!"

"As you wish, Empress," whispered Rolo, advancing further into the chamber.

Suddenly Lazro and Riffa popped up from behind the barricade (bed) and pelted them with wads of colored slime from their oozy-blasters!

"It's a trap!" yelled Rolo.

"You'll never defeat me!" yelled Riffa. "Mwahahaaaa!"

With a din of motorized pumps and cheap sound effects, the air was thick with glowing slime —red, green, purple, and blue—splattering the walls and their clothes in absolute carnage.

"Ug! I've been hit!" groaned Lazro, clutching his chest and falling to the floor, polka-dotted with slime. He looked up at Zira and wheezed, "I'm sorry ... I ... betrayed you ... my empress."

"You were a brave knight, Sir Lazrolot," she said, "but you chose the wrong side!"

"Tell ... my family," wheezed Lazro, convulsing and coughing up imaginary blood, "I ...

love ... them ..." He reached up toward the ceiling light above—then his arm dropped, his eyes fluttered shut, and his tongue flopped out.

Rolo fell to his knees and yelled to the sky with clenched fists, "Noooooo! Not Lazrolot!"

Riffa growled, "Now you both shall meet an even worse fate!" She slimed them mercilessly.

"Retreat!" yelled Zira. "Retreat!"

They scampered back down the hall as Rolo fired green slime randomly behind him without looking.

Riffa chased them into the temple (kitchen) and around the great altar (table), exchanging splats of green, purple, and blue.

"We can't make it, Empress," cried Rolo. "We're out-slimed! We must escape into the sewers!" He dove under the sofa.

"You can't desert me!" yelled Zira, now glazed with slime. She leaped onto the battlement (sofa). "Come back here, Commander Rolo!"

She leaned over the edge and swiped her arm side to side under the sofa until she caught his leg and dragged him out slowly.

"Nooooo! Noooo!" he wailed, giggling.

She lifted him in front of her face, dangling him upside down, and proclaimed her judgment: "Deserters will not be tolerated! So now, Commander, you shall suffer the ultimate punishment: *Juicy kisses!*" She wet her lips, puckered, and wiggled them like big fish lips as she slowly pulled his face closer and closer.

"Nooooo!" he screamed, laughing. "The slobber! Oh, the slobber!"

"I'll avenge you, Rolo!" yelled Lazro from the hallway, apparently recovered from his tragic death. He splatted Zira with red slime.

Before she could retaliate, the drawbridge opened unexpectedly (front door).

"Kids!" bellowed the dragon (their mom), holding a large blizza box. "I've got dinner!"

She looked around the room in dismay. The sofa cushions were strewn across the floor. Glowing slime dripped down the furniture. And the walls. And the ceiling. And her children. "What the quasar have you kids been doing all day? Better get this cleaned up!"

"No problem!" chirped Zira.

The self-cleaning slime was already starting to evaporate. And soon the robo-vacuum was circulating around the house, sucking up the remaining debris and putting everything back in order. But Rolo ran from the loud, terrifying contraption and hid under the sofa. He never did like the robo-vacuum.

Next, they were all sitting around the kitchen table, laughing and eating warm, gooey zepperoni

blizza. Except for Rolo, who was *under* the table, where Zira slipped him scraps when she thought no one was looking.

Zira hummed cheerfully, enjoying her delicious blizza. It had been a wonderful summer day so far. But sadly, she could not foresee that this was the last night they would all be together as a family.

5. Just Another Day

Three more years had passed, and much had changed. Rolo was growing taller, hairier, and smellier (an especially gross but endearing quality of you earthlings). Now today, like on most days, he was home alone, waiting for Zira to return from school.

He lay sprawled out flat on his back in the middle of the family room carpet in the afternoon sun. He had found a ball of yarn to entertain himself and made it a game to see how many times he could toss it from hand to hand without dropping it. But then he forgot to count, so he was just lazily going through the motions.

The house was silent, except for the monotonous ticking of a clock and the muffled buzz from the flish tank. The seven stubby, round flish stared blankly at the yarn ball. They swiveled slightly side to side as the ball arced from Rolo's left hand to right hand, to left hand, to right hand.

Rolo let out a long sigh to express his boredom, but no one was there to hear it. The days on blorx are seventy-seven hours long, but the older he got, the longer they felt. He had already finished his second eight-hour nap for the day, and there was not much else to do when Zira was away —just the same old games and same old toys, which he had outgrown long ago.

He wished to explore the world of wonder outside, to meet up with his earthling friends and roam the neighborhood without any leashes or restrictions. But this was a hopeless wish, because the doors and windows were locked and earthling-proofed with some complex contraption he could never figure out.

He looked up at the ticking wall clock. It was still squiggly-symbol o'clock. Zira and Riffa should be home soon.

Quiggles suddenly made a loud snort-gag-snore. He was Rolo's pet, a green quagling with one big yellow eye, two arms, and three legs, as tall as Rolo's thigh. He was curled on top of his perch in the corner—sleeping, mouth open, tongue out, drooling.

The snort had startled Rolo, and he fumbled the yarn. It bounced off his chest and rolled just out of reach. He gently grasped the tail end of the yarn and pulled it back slowly, but the yarn ball only rolled in place. He pulled faster. Same result. He waited briefly … and then … yanked it suddenly as if to catch it off guard. The yarn ball hopped upward, spinning rapidly and unraveling, till it hit the carpet and rolled away even further. Rolo stared at the frazzled frizz ball for a moment, then strained to reach it—as if he could stretch his arm longer by sheer willpower. It was no use. But still, he felt it wasn't worth the effort to just sit up and grab it.

Finally, something new happened, a noise coming from the entry. Rolo turned his attention to the front door. It was a key unlocking!

6. From Boredom to Bedlam

Rolo scrambled to the entry and crouched behind a large potted plant near the front door. He had a plan.

The door swung open with a whoosh and banged into the wall.

"Rolo, I'm home!" Zira hollered. Her teeth now sparkled with braces, and her hair was longer. She wore her favorite purple hoodie and her magenta backpack, which was covered with cartoonish doodles that she had scrawled during stretches of boredom.

Rolo held his breath and stealthily watched and waited for her to walk past. Left foot ... right foot ... clear! He sprang up and dashed toward the open door, and this time he made it all the way to the front step before Zira's hands caught him around his chest and scooped him up.

"No, no, no, you little sneaker!" she giggled.

He laughed. "Well, it was worth the try."

"Oh, you'll never get away from *me*, 'cause you're *just ... so ... cute!*" She hugged and cradled him too tightly until he groaned and strained to breathe. *"But look at dat cute belly!"* She pressed her mouth on his exposed tummy and blew a big, noisy, wet zerbert. He tried hard not to laugh, but that was impossible. He squirmed uncontrollably and attempted to wiggle out of her grip as she carried him, but that was impossible too.

"Have you been a good boy? Have you?"

"Mmmaybee," he said with a wry smile.

"Guess whaaaaat? It's time for take-off. Ready?"

He tensed up as she swung him back and forth, higher and higher.

"Three ... two ... one ... Weeeeeeee!" She flung him forward and high into the air, arcing all the way across the family room. He squeezed his eyes shut and braced himself as he plummeted into the giant beanbag seat with a smush. He never really liked this game, but he liked that she liked it.

"Wasn't that fun?"

He refrained from replying, and instead let out a muffled moan face-down. It was always a rough transition from boredom to bedlam—from too much quiet to too much chaos.

Next, Riffa trudged through the front door and slammed it. She was now a full-fledged adolescent. She wore dark eyeliner and a piercing in her antenna, partly because it annoyed her mom. And she wore a heavy bomber jacket covered in patches, and a short white skirt, like she was half cold and half warm. She continued her trudge toward the hallway, all while looking down

at her phone and cracking her gum.

Zira skipped toward Rolo as he tried to wiggle out of the mushy beanbag.

"Hey, Riffa, watch Rolo fly again!"

Riffa kept trudging, turning her head just enough to give Zira a snarky side-eye. She popped a bubble, turned back to her phone, and disappeared into the hallway.

Zira stopped short and slumped into the sofa. Rolo was relieved to avoid another tossing. Then she patted the sofa cushion. "C'mere, Rolo Polo. Up up up!"

"Wait, gimme a sec," he said, stalling.

"Oh look, it's food time! I bet you're hungry." She sprang off the sofa and into the kitchen.

He shrugged. "Meh."

It sounded to him like Zira was going out of her way to bang every cabinet at least three times and clap all the utensils together. Then he heard the all-too-familiar mechanical sound of the plasmatic can opener.

Meanwhile, Quiggles was waking up on his perch over the beanbag. After a few bleary eye-blinks, he wiped the drool from his chin.

Rolo looked up to see Quiggles looking down at him from directly overhead.

"Quiggles, don't even think about it," he warned sternly.

But Quiggles stood at the edge and slowly raised his arms overhead.

"Quiggles, dooooon't!"

Then he leaped into a triple-half-back-side-down dive directly toward Rolo.

"Nooo!" Rolo screamed as he saw Quiggles's three-cheek butt rushing toward his face. He rolled out of the way just before Quiggles plopped into the beanbag. Then Quiggles promptly licked Rolo all over his face and mouth.

"Oh!—tphphp—Okay—tphphp—That's enough, Quiggles—tphphp—That's enou—tphphp."

Quiggles abruptly froze mid-lick, tongue still out, looking off into the hall like he heard something. Then, for no obvious reason, he casually hopped off the beanbag and strolled out of the room.

Rolo chuckled. "Bye!" he sarcasticated.

"Okay, come and get it!" yelled Zira from the kitchen, banging a spoon on the side of a can.

Rolo extracted himself from the beanbag, shuffled to his little earthling-sized counter, and sat on the stool. She dangled the can upside down, high over his bowl. A perfect cylinder of gray-brown goop slowly emerged with a slobbery suction sound. He watched without anticipation. The goopy food stalled, clinging to the can, refusing to drop. She shook the can, causing a rhythmic slurping sound. The goop reluctantly crept out, a little more, a little more, then finally fell in free-fall. It landed with a splat in his bowl and jiggled, still in its cylindrical form.

"There you go. I made it myself!" She giggled.

When it finally stopped jiggling, he grabbed his spoon and braced himself. It smelled like ... nothing. Exactly how it tasted. He scooped a small

sample of goopy food (or "foop" as he liked to call it) and tried to swallow it without chewing.

Riffa tromped back from the hallway, holding a long, wooly sweater.

"Hey, Squid Squirt! Your earthling was sleeping on my bed again!"

"I can hear you, you know," mumbled Rolo with foop in his mouth.

"Well, were you?" Riffa interrogated.

"Mmmaybee?" He tried to stifle a smirk.

"Roloooo," Zira scolded, but not really. "Why didn't you sleep in your *own* bed?"

"What, like, for *every* nap? Pff. What's the fun in that? I need variety, keep things fresh!" He beamed a smile, trying to win her over.

Riffa held out her sweater to show Zira the little pajama bottoms stuck on it. "Look, he left his pants on my sweater!" The pajama pants peeled away from the sweater with a crackle of static, then released their tenuous grasp and flopped to the ground.

"So *that's* where they went!" said Rolo. "I was looking all over for those."

Zira rolled her eyes at Riffa. "Oh, you're *so* dramatic!"

"Whatever, Squid Squirt." Riffa turned to go back to her room.

"Hey, Riffa," said Zira, "you wanna play Blorgan Pong with me?"

"What? Ew." Once again, she disappeared down the hall. Then to top it off, she yelled, "And tell your pet to stay out of my room!"

"I can still hear you!" Rolo hollered back with a sly grin.

Riffa was no fun anymore. She seemed annoyed by Zira all the time. And Rolo, too. And their mom. And everyone.

"Hey Riffa?" yelled Zira.

No answer.

"Riffa!"

Long pause.

"Whaaat?!" whined Riffa.

"Rolo has an appointment now at the V-E-T."

"I can spell, you know!" said Rolo. "And that's *next* week, not today," he lied.

Zira smirked at him.

Riffa yelled, "So what?"

"So you need to come with us. You're supposed to be the responsible one while Mom's away this week. Remember?"

Rolo bluffed, "No, I swear. The appointment is *next* week."

Zira chuckled. "You're not fooling me like that again."

"Awww!" He hated the vet.

"Riffa?" yelled Zira.

Nothing.

"Riffa!"

"Fine." Riffa trudged toward the front door, face-down in her phone.

"Then I wanna go to the earthling park after."

Rolo perked up at that.

"Nkay, whatever." Riffa leaned by the door, crossed her legs, and popped a bubble.

Zira said, "Come on, Rolo!"

He abandoned his unfinished foop and hopped off the stool. She put on his harness and leash.

"Come on, Quiggles!" he called out.

Quiggles came galloping from the hall and hopped on Rolo's back, almost knocking him over.

As soon as Riffa opened the door, Rolo ran out at full speed.

"Freeeeedom!" he yelled while dashing across the lawn. The retractable leash unreeled in Zira's hand with a whirring, then a sharp click, jerking Rolo backward onto the lawn and spinning Quiggles into the air. Everyone laughed—except for Riffa, who just snapped her gum.

Rolo's day so far had been boring, chaotic, and very, very ordinary. But by the end of the day, everything will change for Rolo in the most extraordinary way.

7. The Squirler Rivalry

After Rolo's vet appointment, they all walked along the sidewalk through the pleasant suburban neighborhood toward the earthling park. It was a sunny day with a clear yellow sky. Streams of light passed through the blue leaves of the trees lining the street, where blirds quietly gabbed and gossiped amongst themselves. Zira held Rolo's leash attached to his harness, and Rolo held Quiggles's leash, like a little pet train.

Rolo was licking a meat-flavored lollipop that he got from the vet as a bribe for cooperating. Resentfully, he rubbed his arm, which was still sore from the shots. He didn't even have belly worms, so why did Zira make him get shots?! As they passed by a street sign, to spite her, he "accidentally" walked on the wrong side of the pole and passed between Zira's legs, tangling up the leash.

"Rolo! You silly boy," giggled Zira as she untangled the leash.

He gave a rascally smile, and Quiggles chuckled.

"So anyway," Zira continued rambling to Riffa, "then in class we were making these dioramas for quantum tunneling, and Mrs. Glaxoblat said we could decorate it with dark matter if we wanted, but I ran out because I used all mine yesterday on my report cover for antiquarks—Oh, I got an A on that! Well, actually an A negative because I used pencil instead of pen. Anyway, I had neutrino glitter and plasma paste, but I didn't have any more dark matter so I asked her if I could borrow some and she said ..."

I'll spare you the rest of this story since you earthlings don't really understand fifth-grade quantum physics. But it was pretty funny.

Regardless, Riffa wasn't even listening. Instead, she walked behind Zira, looking at her phone as usual.

Meanwhile, as Rolo chomped the last bite of his meat-flavored lollipop, an acorn fell on his head. He brushed it off. Then another one hit him. He looked up and saw a squirler high in a tree, grinning at him mischievously.

Then another acorn hit him, and he saw there was a second squirler. And a third. And a fourth and fifth.

"Hey!" he shouted up to the rambunctious rogents.

The five squirlers chucked another volley of acorns on him.

"Hey! Stop that!"

The squirlers cackled squeakily. Quiggles growled at them.

"Rolo, stop yelling," Zira scolded.

Another squirler pelted Rolo in the back of the head.

He turned and shouted, "Stop that! Stop!"

No one knows exactly when the rivalry started between squirlers and earthlings. It is simply a fact of nature that all earthlings hate squirlers, and all squirlers hate earthlings. Plus, there was that one time Rolo trapped a squirler in the backyard and brought it inside as a gift for Zira. But for some reason, instead of thanking him, Zira just screamed and tossed the both of them outside.

Zira yanked on his leash. "Rolo, shush! Now be good and come on."

"But look," he whined, pointing up into the trees. "They're throwing nuts at me."

Zira looked up. Instantly, all the squirlers fluffed up their big, bushy, orange-striped tails, enlarged their bright, shiny eyes, and nibbled away at acorns in their little paws.

"Aww," gushed Zira. "They're so cute! They're harmless."

"No, they're—"

"Rolo, leave the poor little squirlers alone," she said sternly.

As soon as Zira looked away, all the squirlers reverted back to their evil grins. One flicked another acorn on Rolo's head and stuck out its tongue.

Quiggles glared at the squirlers and made rude hand gestures.

Rolo sighed, and they continued toward the park.

8. Cut the Leash

Off in one corner of the earthling park, a small group of blorxlings were protesting. They were animal rights activists, wearing tie-dyed tee shirts and headbands with flowers in their hair. They waved cardboard signs like "Earthlings Have Rights Too," and they chanted in rhythm:

> *Cut* the *leash*.
> *Set* them *free*.
> *Earth*-lings *are* like *you* and *me!*

> *Cut* the *leash*.
> *Let* them *be*.
> *Earth*-lings *need* e-*qua*-li-*ty!*

Zira and Riffa did not seem to notice—there were always protesters there for one cause or another. And they never mattered to Rolo before, but this time they caught his attention because they were actually protesting about earthlings. He listened closer.

Until this moment, he had never really wondered *why* he was a pet. All his life, he had been a pet. And all the other earthlings too. And all the generations before them, and before them. But was it always that way? Why did no one ever talk about that? Was it a secret? The more he thought, the more unanswered questions sparked in his mind.

"Hey Zira? Where do earthlings come from?"

"Oh. Uhhhh." She hesitated. "Well, when a mommy earthling and a daddy earthling love each other very much—"

"No, no-no-no! I mean where were *all* earthlings from originally? Like what continent, Blorfrica? Blurope? Blasia?"

"Oh. I dunno. Lemme see."

Zira concentrated and her brain-chip started flashing. All blorxlings have a cybernetic chip on their foreheads under their skin, which they use to look up information, do calculations, and store their old memories. Lights blinked in a diamond pattern on her forehead as she searched for the answer. She cocked her antennae curiously and tapped her brain-chip. "Hmm. That's weird."

"What's the matter?"

"Well, I'm searching online all over the nebula, but I can't find any information."

"Huh. Is your chip broken?"

"No, I can find any other topic. I just can't find anything about where earthlings are from. Riffa, do you know?"

"Know what?" she said flatly without looking.

"Where earthlings come from?"

"Why would I know that?"

"Can you check, please?"

Riffa sighed, barely looking up from her phone. Her chip flashed for a few seconds. "Nope, nothing there." She looked back down at her phone.

"That's really strange," said Zira. Then she shrugged it off like it was no big deal.

But it was a big deal, and Rolo couldn't stop thinking about it. Where did earthlings come from? And how did they live before they were pets?

9. The Earthling Park

Zira led the way to the play area in the earthling park. Inside the fence on the lush purple grass, earthlings frolicked off-leash, from the young earthling pups to the fully grown adults. The more senior earthlings ambled around the border, chatting with each other. In the corner, two earthlings ran through an agility course—obstacles of ramps, tunnels, high jumps, and weave poles. Outside the fence, blorxlings sat on benches supervising. There were regular drinking fountains for blorxlings, and little drinking fountains for earthlings. A seeing-eye earthling led their blind blorxling along the path.

Zira opened the gate for Rolo and Quiggles, then detached Rolo's leash while he detached Quiggles's leash. She pulled a large, bright blorple flying disc from her backpack. (Blorple is a color you earthlings cannot see, so it just looks gray to you.) "Okay, Rolo, ready to play some blizbee?"

Rolo saw two of his earthling friends hanging out nearby. He waved to them. "Can't I go see my friends first?"

"Oh, c'mon. You like blizbee!" insisted Zira.

Unenthusiastically, he complied. "Okay."

Zira curled her arm back and did a big fake throw, sneakily tucking the blizbee behind her back. "Go get it! There it goes!" She pointed out to the field, trying to stifle a giggle.

Rolo didn't even turn his head. "Nice try. Never gets old."

"Hey Riffa," Zira called out, "come play blizbee with us!"

Riffa was leaning against a lamppost outside the fence. She looked up from her phone, rolled her eyes, and looked back down.

Zira's smile faded. They used to play blizbee together all the time, Lazro too. But that was before Riffa turned so sulky. Zira missed those years, back when they were all together, before that one dark night. But at least she still had Rolo.

She and Rolo threw the blizbee back and forth in the sunlight. Rolo managed a few trick shots, even though the blizbee was awkwardly too big for him, and Quiggles sometimes sat on top for a dizzy flying-saucer ride. Until Zira accidentally threw it too high over Rolo's head.

"Oops! Sorry."

He trotted to where it landed by an amber-trunk tree, which happened to be where his earthling friends were hanging out.

"Rolo!" they cheered.

10. Maybe Something More

"How ya doing?" Yoola greeted Rolo. She was short, energetic, and hard not to like.

"Hey Yoola! Hula Yoola ... Uvula Yoola ..." Rolo was trying to think of something funny to rhyme, but failing.

"Uvula?" she teased with a smirk, then gave him a big hug.

Smuffins bumped fists with Rolo. "What up, dawg?" He was Rolo's best friend, a big guy for his age, already growing a wispy mustache. He always seemed to be scowling, which looked quite intimidating. But that was just how his face normally looked. Inside he was a warm softy.

"Hey, Smuffins, the muffin man!" said Rolo.

Smuffins approved with his scowly version of a smile. "Alright, that works, that works."

Yoola and Smuffins were dressed in matching green tracksuits. They lived together across the street with the same owners.

Yoola pointed to Rolo's harness. "Is that new?"

"Yeah, Zira took me shopping at the pet store yesterday."

"Looks good."

"Well ..." Rolo shrugged.

"You don't like it?"

"I woulda preferred the blue one."

"Why didn't you get it?"

"I dunno. She really liked this one."

Smuffins chimed in. "Dude, you jus' gotta tell her what you want."

Rolo mocked, "This advice coming from a guy with a big pink bow?"

Indeed, Smuffins had a large pink bow on top of his hair, which certainly helped to soften his intimidating face. He shrugged. "I pick my battles. Besides, it makes my girl happy. She's good to me." He nodded at his owner sitting on the bench, a blorxlingette younger than Zira. She waved back at him enthusiastically.

Zira then jogged up to the group and greeted them in a sugary voice. "Well hello there, earthies! Found your little friend, huh?" She patted Yoola and Smuffins on their heads. "Rolo, do you need to go potty?"

He dropped his face into his hand in utter embarrassment and covered his eyes, as if no one else could see him that way. Through gritted teeth, he mumbled, "Zira! Go away. You're embarrassing me!"

"Okay, fine. I'll be back in a sec." She attached his leash and tied the handle to the tree. "Have fun with your little friends. And be good!"

Rolo closed his eyes even tighter and grimaced.

Yoola chuckled as Zira jogged away. "You have such a cute owner."

Another one of their friends, Fabli, strutted up behind them. He was the oldest of the group, in peak physical condition. His hair was long and wavy and dyed excessively blonde. His skin was tanned to a dark bronze, and his teeth somehow shined whiter than white. He was raised and groomed as a show earthling, and he always managed to slip his championship titles into any conversation.

"Hellooo," he said in an exotic, suave accent.

Rolo said, "Hey, Fabli. Bobbly ... nobbly ..." Again, he couldn't think of a good rhyme.

"Yo, Fabli!" cheered Yoola as she gave him a big hug.

"Hey, careful of de hair! I've got a big show tomorrow."

"Oh wow, which one?" she asked.

"De Blorxminster Kennel Club. I've got a good shot at best-in-show dis year."

Rolo was happy to be here at the park with his friends (despite his embarrassing owner). Even if they were merely chit-chatting, it was the first time in almost a week that he got to hang out with other earthlings—peers who understood him and talked to him as equals, not talking down to him the way blorxlings always did.

He asked Yoola, "So, what have you been up to?"

"Let's see. On Blaturday we went on a walk. And on Blunday we went on a walk. Oh, and I switched to a new food, which is pretty exciting. So it's been a pretty good week so far!"

"Nice," he said, just to be polite. Her routine was as boring as his, yet she seemed content, even happy, which was puzzling to him.

Smuffins added, "And I got a new pet toy for my birthday. It's one of those hover drones that shoots laser pointers. It's pretty cool," he bragged with a scowly grin.

Yoola teased, "I dunno about that. It looks dangerous to me. I don't like going near that thing."

"Nah, you jus' jealous."

"Ha! You just wish you had my automatic ball launcher!"

"Oh puh-lease. That thing's not even close! No contest."

Fabli changed the topic back to his competitions. "I've been doing my training, getting my agility times down for de show. And I went to de groomer today." Somehow the breeze was always gently blowing through his flowing hair.

Yoola asked, "How about you, Rolo?"

"Oh, same ol'. Naps, snacks, the usual. I guess I shouldn't complain. But, uh ..." He hesitated. "Can I ask you all something? Like, don't you ever wonder if maybe there's something more?"

"More what?" Yoola asked.

"Like more we should be *doing*."

Smuffins thought about this for a moment. "Like ... car rides?"

"No, I mean, I dunno, more than just playing and being taken care of?"

Yoola looked perplexed. "What's wrong with that?"

Rolo didn't know how to answer that, so he just said, "Nothing."

Fabli asked skeptically, "Are you on any new medications?"

"What else is there, dawg?" said Smuffins. "We're safe, we're healthy, we're well fed. And they give us cool toys and we can chill all day. Nothing else we need, right?"

Rolo contemplated this, but it still didn't feel right.

Yoola asked, "What's the matter, Rolo? Is your body going through changes and now you're having deep, philosophical thoughts?" She giggled.

He blushed and smiled. "Mmmaybee ... But ... don't you ever wonder where we came from?"

"I came from a champion breeder," boasted Fabli.

"No, before that. Like someplace earthlings lived in the wild, where we ran around hunting and taking care of ourselves?"

Yoola sneered in repulsion. "Like those packs of stray street earthlings? Outside?! Gross."

Smuffins squinted at him. "You don't hunt!"

"Well, no. Bad example," Rolo admitted. "But maybe I would if I had the choice."

Fabli tried to be helpful. "You could go into competitions."

Rolo thought about how much exercise that would require—way too much.

"Dawg, I don't know what you worrying about. Life has always been this good. We got it made! You should be happy with what you got."

Rolo sighed. "I know I should, but ..."

During all this talk, Rolo had unbuckled his harness to scratch an itch. Unfortunately, that got the attention of two robots patrolling the park: earthling catchers. They looked like military machines, painted tan with the "Animal Control Force" logo on their backs. They were much bigger than earthlings, about the size of blorxlings, but Private B-L1 was tall and thin, and Private B-D3 was short and squat. They rolled up to the group.

Private B-D3 confronted Rolo, speaking in a military staccato. "Earthling, civil code 473-dash-7 requires you to wear a harness or collar at all times in public."

Private B-L1 commanded, "All of you, identify your owners now."

Yoola, Smuffins, and Fabli each pointed to their owners. Rolo looked around for Zira while fumbling to re-buckle his harness.

B-L1 prodded him. "Where is your owner, earthling?"

"Um, she was just here, but I don't see her—"

"Civil code 314-dash-9 requires earthlings to be under direct supervision of their owners or wranglers at all times in public."

"Let's see your identification tag."

Nervously, Rolo pulled out the ID tag he wore around his neck.

B-L1 scanned it and looked up his records. "It says here your pet license is expired. Your owner needed to renew this on Bleptember 40th. And I see you've got a prior for chasing squirlers. *And* it says you were never neutered."

"Neutered!" Rolo exclaimed with wide eyes.

"Civil code 518-dash-1."

"That is a class 2 violation," said B-L1. "Looks like we're going to have to take you in now."

11. The Blorxian Subway

"Come with us," commanded Private B-L1.

Private B-D3 slid open a panel door in his wide, hollow belly, which served as a holding cell to carry Rolo back to the Animal Control Force compound.

Rolo froze as B-L1 reached out his mechanical grabbers. Fear spun in his mind but went nowhere, paralyzing him with indecision.

But then Quiggles decided for him. He leaped up and kicked Rolo out of the way. Without thinking, Rolo started running, only to be yanked back by his harness. He was still leashed to the tree.

"I got yo back, dawg!" Smuffins helped Rolo out of his harness while Quiggles kicked grass at the two bots.

Rolo then ran around the tree, leading the bots in a circular chase. Their wheels tore up the purple grass as they tried to grab him. During their second lap, Smuffins hooked the harness onto one of the bots, tethering him to the tree. Yoola took her leash out of her pocket and tangled it around the other bot's foot wheels. They were now immobilized, at least for the moment.

Rolo and Smuffins ran away at full speed, but in no particular direction. Quiggles held the defensive line, staying behind to taunt and distract the bots to give Rolo a good head start.

"Where's Zira?" panted Rolo. "Do you see her?"

"No," huffed Smuffins.

While he didn't see her, from across the park, she saw him ... *and* the bots now chasing him, swerving and weaving around the crowd.

"Rolo!" yelled Zira. But he couldn't hear her.

She ran to Riffa. "Help me! We have to catch Rolo!"

Riffa looked up from her phone, blew a bubble, then looked back down.

Rolo and Smuffins ran toward a gate, but it was closed and the latch was earthling-proof. They panicked as the bots closed in.

Luckily, a blorxling was now entering the gate, so they slipped through.

Quiggles dashed across the grass toward Riffa, sprang off the fence, and snatched her phone from her hand, drawing her into the chase. Quaglings are very perceptive, and he had an uncanny sense that she would be needed in the consequential events that were soon to ensue. He deflated her giant phone down to a mini-phone while he bounded away.

"Quiggles! I need that!" exploded Riffa as she chased after him—or more importantly, her phone.

"Where we running?" huffed Smuffins.

Rolo saw a subway station outside the park. "Here. In here!"

They ran into the subway with Quiggles close behind, followed by the earthling catchers, who were followed by Riffa and Zira.

Inside the subway station, a small crowd of blorxlings waited on the platform. A sign overhead read, "Next wormhole in 10 ... 9 ... 8 ..."

Rolo, Smuffins, and Quiggles reached the platform just as a wormhole opened with a burst of pink light. They hopped inside and ran to a forward seat, and nervously waited for the wormhole to close.

The bots reached the platform and sped toward the wormhole. B-L1 rolled inside just before it snapped shut. Rolo and Smuffins gasped.

The inside of the wormhole looked like a streaked tube of pinkish light. Passengers stood in the aisle and sat in the seats. A sign overhead displayed the next stop: Blorzington Station.

The bot rolled up the aisle toward them.

"Hang on!" said Rolo as he hit a button on their seat. The wormhole forked in two, and their seat veered into the left tube.

The bot followed.

Back at the station, B-D3 rolled into a separate wormhole, and Zira and Riffa hopped into a third wormhole to find Rolo before the bots could catch him.

Just as B-L1 was about to reach Rolo and Smuffins's seat, Rolo hit the button again, and so did Smuffins, causing the wormhole to fork twice rapidly, leading the bot into the wrong tube while they escaped.

"Wait, where are we?" Rolo looked up at the sign. "Was that Bluxian? Blazian? Blorian?" Rolo had ridden the subway with Zira many times before, so he thought maybe he could find his way back home, but the station names all looked the same to him. (These names are obviously distinct and easy to remember, but not for your little earthling brains.)

Rolo and Smuffins looked around, hoping to find a subway map.

Suddenly, a tube merged from behind, and B-D3 steamed toward them. They yelped and took another exit. But now in this new tube, B-L1 stood ahead of them, waiting. They quickly exited again, and luckily, by chance, Zira and Riffa were now sitting across the aisle.

"Rolo, there you are!" Zira exclaimed.

Rolo looked up and down the wormhole. "Are they gone?"

But once again, a tube merged with the unrelenting bots.

Rolo and the others hopped out at the next station and ran across the platform. A 3D holographic globe hovered in the air—a map of all the wormhole lines crisscrossing the planet, not over the surface, but straight through the mantle and core. One line even connected to the moon.

They all ran inside another wormhole.

"Rolo, you poor thing!" cried out Zira. "Are you okay?"

But before he could answer, each bot merged behind and in front of them and closed in. They yelped and exited, but in the confusion, Rolo lost Zira again.

He knew they would surely be caught if they stayed in the subway much longer.

"C'mon," said Smuffins, "we gotta get outta here."

12. Old Blorgton

Old Blorgton was dirty, dingy, and dilapidated. Litter tumbled down the streets and alleys in the warm breeze. Weeds grew from the cracks in the sidewalks and pavement, and the few trees were bare of leaves. Many of the buildings were abandoned, with broken windows and walls covered with graffiti that looked like crop circles. Few inhabitants went outside in this neighborhood, and those who did kept to themselves and kept their heads down.

In front of a bus-stop bench, a wormhole opened over the sidewalk with a pink glow. Rolo, Smuffins, and Quiggles hopped out of the hole, ran into a nearby alley, and crouched behind a dumpster, watching to see if the bots would follow. Several long seconds later, the wormhole closed.

Rolo felt relieved. But once he looked around and realized just how lost they were, that relief reverted to worry.

"Where are we?" asked Smuffins.

"Good question."

They stepped out of the alley and looked up and down the street. Quiggles curiously sniffed the lampposts.

Rolo noticed the sign floating over the bus stop, counting down: "Next wormhole in 94,426 … 94,425 … 94,424 …"

"Uh oh," he said. "That was the last wormhole today. The next one isn't till tomorrow."

"What?! How we gonna get home now?!"

"Shhh, shh, shh!" Rolo saw a hulking, grungy rogent with matted fur shuffling out of the alley. It bared its yellow teeth and growled at them. Quiggles growled back. It grumbled and shook its head, and shuffled along.

"Okay," said Smuffins, "maybe we jus' wait here for your owner to find us."

"How? That wormhole is closed till tomorrow."

"Oh yeah. Well, maybe we can find another subway station to get back home, right?"

"Yeah, I guess so," said Rolo. "But then the bots will just catch us in the subway."

"But there're probably more earthling catchers here in the city too." Smuffins made a good point.

Fear sank in. Rolo always wanted to escape home and go explore on his own, roaming the streets with no leash and no rules—at least for a little while. But this was not what he had hoped. He wanted to get back to the comfort and security of home. And he wanted to get back to Zira. He now felt guilty. He knew how much she loved him, and how much she just wanted to play with him, but he was always resistant, maybe a little too bratty. Maybe he wasn't appreciative enough.

Then his thoughts were interrupted by impending danger: An Animal Control Force tank hovering down the street toward them.

"Hide!" Rolo hissed. They rushed back into the alley and ducked behind the dumpster. The large, blocky tank rumbled steadily past.

"You're right," said Rolo, "the longer we stay here, they'll probably just catch us."

"Okay," said Smuffins, "so let's go see where we can find another subway."

13. The Search Begins

Meanwhile, a few blocks away, another wormhole opened at a different bus stop. Zira and Riffa hopped out and looked around.

"Do you see them?" Zira asked desperately.

She was worried about so many things that could go wrong. Rolo was lost. He had gotten off leash before, but never so far from home. What if the earthling catchers found him and took him away and locked him up in a compound? What if he kept running and got even more lost? What if he couldn't find food or water? What if he got hit by a car? Or attacked by street earthlings? Or if a stranger took him and kept him as their own pet? Or worse, what if he met another blorxling he liked better?!

Riffa read the bus stop sign counting down. "Wait, that was the last wormhole! Ugh, thanks a lot, Squid Squirt!"

"What are you mad at *me* for?!"

"Because now we're stuck here because of you and your annoying earthling!"

"It's not my fault! They were gonna take him away!"

"And his stupid pet took my phone. Ugh!"

"C'mon, Riffa, you need to help me find him! He's lost and probably so scared. If we don't find him soon, the bots will catch him and take him away!"

"How is that *my* problem?"

Zira mumbled just loud enough for Riffa to hear, "Lazro would've helped me."

"Yeah, well Lazro's not here!" Riffa shot back.

"Why are you so mean, Riffa?!" Zira was angry, and hurt, and scared, and frustrated—all at once. But she needed her sister's help. She paused for a moment and tried again. "Please, we need to find Rolo ... Please?"

Riffa took a long breath. "Fine. We know they got off at one of these wormhole stops, so they can't be far."

"Oh wait, I have an idea!" Zira took a gizmo from her backpack, pressed a few buttons, and pointed it at a lamppost. A holographic poster appeared with the word "LOST" in big letters and a photo of Rolo.

They started walking in an arbitrary direction, while Zira called out repeatedly, "Rolooo!"

14. The Animal Control Force

The Animal Control Force Command Center buzzed with busy bots working at their consoles. The vast room was dark and windowless, with rows of robo-tech computers. Rolo's photo was featured on one of the large monitors spanning the walls.

Colonel C-4 yelled at Privates B-L1 and B-D3. "If it isn't Beezledum and Beezledee! Now do you two bolt buckets want to tell me how you managed to lose a mangy mutt in a subway?!"

The colonel was a stocky bot with a gruff voice, and some appendage sticking out the side of his mouth that looked like a lit cigar.

The privates stood stiffly at attention, their optical sensors aligned straight forward.

Ever since the robot wars ended long ago, the poor bots had nothing else to do, so the blorxian government assigned them a menial task that no one else wanted: animal control. In hindsight, that may have been a big mistake.

A corporal bot interrupted. "Colonel, we are getting reports of a possible match—a feral juvenile male shorthair earthling in Old Blorgton, heading east."

"Sergeant!" yelled the colonel. "Get me satellite surveillance on the eastern seaboard, sector B41."

"Yes sir!"

"Corporal!" yelled the colonel. (Actually, he always yelled.) "Put the surveillance camera feeds on-screen for all blocks north of Bluxenblorg."

"Yes sir!"

"Lieutenant! Scramble the 5th Airborne Drone Squadron. How long till they can intercept?"

The lieutenant checked the console. "Sir, the 5th Squadron is already engaged in sector S95, for the blippo-potamoose stampede, sir."

"Then who do we have available?"

"Sir, Squadron 14 is available, base sector G51, sir."

"G51? Well, that'll have to do. Get them airborne ASAP!"

"Yes sir."

"We need bolts on the ground. Who have we got in that region?"

"The 2nd Platoon is ready in sector C15, sir."

"2nd Platoon? That the best we got? What about the 7th Platoon?"

"They're deployed to the flemming flood in E17."

"9th Platoon?" the colonel ask-yelled.

"Toilet grators."

"1st Platoon?"

"Shnarknado containment."

"Okay, then, we'll have to settle for the 2nd Platoon. Deploy them."

"Yes sir."

The colonel squinted up at Rolo's photo on the monitor, put his hands on his hip servos, and yelled quietly to himself, "You may have won this battle, you cunning cur, but you are no match for the full might of the Animal Control Force!"

15. Pet Vortex

Rolo and Smuffins trekked through Old Blorgton in search of a subway station to get back home. They wandered along the cracked sidewalks between the neglected buildings and littered gutters, bearing the burning sun on their backs and enduring the wafting whiffs of warm garbage. Quiggles, however, was unfazed by the foul heat as he zigzagged ahead and eagerly sniffed the assorted scents layered on each lamppost.

A blorxling woman crossed their path, staring at them suspiciously. Strays were not supposed to be wandering around, and they were already wanted fugitives with the earthling catchers on their trail. Rolo lowered his head to avoid attention. But when Smuffins looked up at her with his naturally scowly face, she stepped aside and let them pass. Luckily, most other blorxlings ignored them.

So far, Rolo and Smuffins had passed a hardware store, butcher shop, clothing store, mattress store, robot repair shop, hovercar supply store, bakery, and another clothing store, but no subway. Then Rolo noticed something ahead that sparked an interesting idea. It was a store sign that read:

PET VORTEX

For the Lesser Species We Love

"Hey Smuffins, look. I think that's a pet store."

"So? You need somethin'?"

"Well, I've been wondering where earthlings come from, and they know about pets, so they'd probably know, right?"

"What're you gettin' at?"

"Let's go inside for a minute so I can ask them a question."

"What? We got no time for that. We gotta get home!"

"C'mon. It'll just take a second," Rolo pleaded.

Smuffins took a long, skeptical breath, but he gave in.

Rolo looked around to make sure no one was watching. He reached for the door handle, but it was too high. So Smuffins lifted him up on his shoulders, and Quiggles climbed on top of Rolo's head. Trying not to look suspicious, the three pets, stacked as one, pulled open the door and slipped inside.

Smuffins made a break for one of the aisles.

"You can put me down now," said Rolo.

"Oh yeah."

With so many different foods and animals, the pet store smelled like a homey concoction that reminded Rolo of his early childhood.

They followed the sounds of blird squawks and squeaky shlamster wheels to another aisle. On the shelves were rows of glass enclosures displaying a diverse collection of domestic wildlife.

First were the preptiles: glizards, griggums, flogs, slurtles, slakes, and slipples. Then the rogents: shmice, shlamsters, boundos, and blabbits. Quiggles hopped onto the shelves and tapped the glass; the animals glared at him. They passed the flerrets, flurfles, oslossums, kiffies, dorgies, and squawklings. Quiggles made faces at them; they made faces back and stuck out their tongues.

"Quiggles, stop that!" Rolo said in a hushed voice.

Quiggles obeyed, but not before shooting his tongue out at one last dorgy.

They passed more enclosures: gruntlings, blabblings, and earthlings. The first earthling enclosure had twin girls sleeping on a couch. One of the girls was twitching, probably dreaming of running, with her foot sticking in the other girl's face. In the second enclosure, a man sat on a couch with a bowl in his lap, popping crunchy kibble into his mouth, with brown crumbs on his fingers and his shirt, and the couch, and the floor.

"Hey," said the man, muffled through the glass.

"Hey," said Rolo, pausing awkwardly, then moving on.

A store clerk walked by, a round blorxling woman with big hair, wearing a red smock. "Whoa, now how did you two rascals get out?"

She reached down for Rolo, but he stepped back, and Smuffins scampered behind a display stand. Quiggles strolled back to the dorgies to continue making faces at them.

"No, no, no," Rolo protested. "We're, uh, we're here with our owner. She just went over there." He pointed vaguely toward the back of the store.

"Oh, well aren't you a cute one!" The clerk knelt down and rubbed Rolo's belly. He allowed it.

"Hey, um, can I ask you a question?"

"Wow, you wanna ask me a question?" Earthlings weren't usually this bold with strangers. "Whatchya wanna know?"

"Yeah, uh, we were wondering," he stammered, "do you know where we came from? I mean earthlings. Where earthlings came from? Like what country?"

"Oh, I did my third-grade thesis on this, dontcha know! We don't actually know where you're from. All we know is that you're not native here."

"What do you mean?"

"I mean you're not Blorxian. Earthlings have a completely different genetic structure, only a *double* helix."

Rolo wasn't sure if he understood. "So we were ... engineered?"

"No, no, I mean earthlings aren't originally from this planet."

"Wait, what? You mean I'm ... *an alien?!*" Rolo was stupefied.

"Well, yah, you all are." She said it like it was obvious.

Smuffins slowly leaned out from behind the display stand. "Say whaaa'?"

"Actually," continued the clerk, "earthlings are considered an invasive species."

Rolo's mouth hung open while he tried to process this unreal reality.

Smuffins said in a hushed voice, "Ask her which planet."

"Oh yeah. Which planet?"

She shrugged. "Not even from our solar system, dontcha know. We don't really know where."

"Oh. Why doesn't anyone know?"

"Well, aren't you just full of questions!" She smiled. "That's the mystery, ya see. There's just no records. But ya know what, I betcha the science museum has some old historical records. It's only a couple blocks that way." She stood up and pointed out the window with her antenna. "I could show your owner. But now, where are they?" She turned to look around the shop. "You two really shouldn't be wandering around off-leash."

But when she looked back down, Rolo, Smuffins, and Quiggles were gone. They had snuck over to the next aisle and were scurrying toward the door. But first, Quiggles halted in front of a tall display of pet treats, pointing to them and jumping excitedly. Rolo scanned for witnesses, and seeing none, he reached up and grabbed a bag.

The clerk turned the corner and spotted them in the act. "Now what do you think you little rascals are doing?" She hobbled after them.

They rushed down the aisle, pushed their way out the glass door, and dashed down the sidewalk.

The clerk stood in the doorway and watched them run away. "Why, those little bandits!"

16. Rolo's Deal

"So now you're stealin' too?" said Smuffins. "Ain't we already in enough trouble?"

Rolo enthusiastically ignored him. "C'mon, this way!"

They trotted across the street in the direction of the museum that the clerk had mentioned. Rolo tore open the bag of contraband pet treats.

"Want one?"

Smuffins squinted indecisively at the bag, then grabbed two treat sticks and bit them both. Rolo tossed Quiggles a treat and took one for himself.

"So we're actually aliens?" mused Rolo. "Isn't that weird? Like, *'Take me to your leader.'*" He chuckled.

Reluctantly, Smuffins chuckled too. He imitated an alien voice: *"We come in peace."*

Quiggles joined in, squawking like a monotone alien with his arms and legs out stiffly.

Rolo asked, "What do you think our planet is like? Do you think earthlings are still there?"

Smuffins scoffed. "That'd be weird. Like livin' in their own lil houses, goin' to lil schools, goin' on walks whenever they want, takin' themselves on car rides."

Rolo chuckled. "Yeah. That kinda sounds nice, actually."

"Talkin' in some weird alien language, prob'ly runnin' round naked and dirty, covered with parasites, and hunted by wild animals," added Smuffins.

The smile fell from Rolo's face.

With a burst of excitement, Smuffins pointed ahead. "Look, there's a sign to the subway!"

Panic fluttered in Rolo's heart. "No, we need to go to the museum first!"

"What?! You crazy?"

He gave a wry smile. "Mmmaybee."

"Those earthling catchers wanna take you away! And our owners gotta be so worried about us! *I'm* worried about us. And dinner is in two hours!"

"But I wanna find out more about our planet!"

"Find out when we get home!"

"I can't," Rolo whined in frustration. "Zira can't find that information online. This is my only chance."

"Then ask her to take you to the museum."

"She'd just say no. She never really listens to what *I* want to do."

"I don't get you, dawg."

"Look, there won't be any earthling catchers in the museum, and it's gotta be close to the subway, so what's the harm?"

Smuffins squinted at him skeptically.

"C'mon," said Rolo, "you're my best friend."

"Oh, so now you play the guilt card?"

But Rolo could see it worked, because now Smuffins was only half angry. Rolo gave a pleading look.

Smuffins sighed and gave in. "*Ten* minutes in the museum. And then we go home. Deal?"

"Deal!"

17. Sing With Me

"Rolooo!" Zira called out. Riffa trailed along silently as they crisscrossed the city in search of poor, lost Rolo. Zira pointed her gizmo at a lamppost and zapped up another holographic lost poster.

Even though they were lost themselves, part of Zira felt happy to be here. This was the longest time she and Riffa had spent together in years, just the two of them, like when they were younger.

"Hey Riffa, remember when me and you hid Rolo in the laundry basket?"

"So you know quantum physics but you don't know grammar?"

"Fine—remember when *you and I* hid Rolo? And he jumped out and scared Lazro?"

"No," said Riffa flatly.

More silence.

Then Zira started singing, "*Atomically the bond that we connect is no anomaly* ... Riffa, sing with me."

Riffa shrugged her off.

Zira resumed singing, skipping around Riffa and tugging on her jacket. "*Elementally, with empathy, it's the nucleus of family.*"

Riffa rolled her eyes.

Zira pointed her gizmo at Riffa and zapped a poster onto her chest, laughing.

"Don't," Riffa groaned and tore off the poster.

Zira skipped more laps around Riffa, zapping several more posters on her. *"Life can be unpredictably a nebulous pressure of intensity."*

"Zira, stop it!"

Zira zapped a poster onto Riffa's face. Riffa yanked it, but it tore in half, leaving only the top half of Rolo's face tacked on her forehead.

"Stop it, Squid Squirt!"

Zira laughed hysterically at the half-Rolo, half-Riffa talking face. Riffa grunted and tore off the half poster. Zira pointed the gizmo at her again, but Riffa quickly slapped it out of her hand.

"I said stop!"

Zira felt the sting on her hand. "Ow, you hurt me!" She held out her hand limply and looked up at Riffa, seeking pity.

Riffa tore off the rest of the posters.

Zira waited for an apology. "Well?"

Riffa sneered at her and said sarcastically, "Sorry!"

Zira dropped her eyes and mumbled, "No you're not."

She knelt to pick up her gizmo off the sidewalk, when by luck, she happened to see Rolo and Smuffins just half a block ahead of them.

"There they are! *Rolo!*"

At a distance, Rolo turned and looked directly at her, then ran away.

18. The Abandoned Warehouse

"Smuffins, run!"

As much as Rolo wanted to go home, he wasn't ready, not yet. So he ran from Zira and Riffa, who were half a block away and closing fast.

But Smuffins just stood in place, smiling. "They can take us home now!"

Rolo halted, frustrated. "But we need to find the museum first!"

"Rolo, think this through, dawg. Why's this so important?"

This question stumped Rolo. He realized there was no particular reason to learn about the earthling planet. What was the point? And yet, it felt so important, at least to himself. He was certain. "I don't ... I can't explain it. I just need to know."

Zira and Riffa were almost at the corner. "Rolo!"

Quiggles tugged on Smuffins.

"Besides," said Rolo, "we had a deal!"

"Rolo!" yelled Zira.

Smuffins groaned. "Yeah, we had a deal."

So they ran.

Quiggles led the way, turning down a narrow alley. They dodged dumpsters and debris while

Quiggles did acrobatic parkour stunts with his five limbs, just to show off. But Zira and Riffa were getting closer.

They turned onto a crowded sidewalk. Here they had the advantage. They were small enough to weave around and between the bustling blorxlings' legs, where they could not be seen. But also, they could not see how close Zira was.

They turned onto another street, where they came across an old, abandoned warehouse. They ran inside the open doorway and hid against the wall, panting.

Rolo stood on his tiptoes to spy out a dirty window. Zira and Riffa ran past.

"Rolo!" Zira called.

He held his breath.

"Rolooo!" she whined. "Where did they go?! Do you see them?"

Riffa shrugged.

"Rolo! C'mere, boy."

Zira turned back toward the warehouse.

"Let's hide!" Rolo whispered hoarsely.

They ducked behind a cluster of old barrels.

Zira stepped inside the warehouse. "Rolo?" she yelled. Her voice reverberated in the vastness till it faded to silence.

Time seemed too slow as Rolo waited for her to leave—or grab him.

Zira groaned.

Then finally, he heard her footsteps recede out the doorway.

The abandoned warehouse was an open emptiness, with tall columns lifting the roof high overhead. The hollowness echoed with nothing inside but a pile of wooden pallets, a few battered barrels in one corner, and bits of litter strewn in scattered heaps. All the doors were torn off their hinges. The windows were cracked or shattered. It was dirty. And yet it was quiet, peaceful. Thickets of flowering foliage grew from cracks in the floor and climbed the columns, breathing life into the air. Sunbeams shined from the skylights, slanting through the haze to touch the colorful graffiti on the walls, giving the space an unexpected warmth and glow.

Rolo peeked out the doorway to double-check. "Okay, they're gone."

"This is crazy," huffed Smuffins, still trying to catch his breath. "I've never run so much my whole life!" He and Quiggles crossed to a stack of pallets to sit and rest. "You got any more of those snacks?"

Rolo smirked and tossed him the bag.

Quiggles inflated Riffa's giant phone and chuckled. Rolo looked over and saw he had apparently snapped a selfie in the subway, with the bot in the background charging them, Rolo's face in a state of terror, and Quiggles up close, making a goofy face.

"Very funny, Quiggles," he sarcasticated. He took the phone, deflated it, and tucked it into his pocket.

Rolo was eager to move on, but Smuffins was sprawled on his back. "You ready to go now?"

"Let's jus' rest here a bit more, 'kay?" said Smuffins, still chewing his treat.

Rolo was too excited to feel tired. His curiosity fueled him.

"Okay. I'll try to see where the museum is."

He speed-walked to the back doorway to survey the area. Outside was an alley lined with dumpsters, garbage cans, boxes, pallets, heaps of garbage, and a curled-up old mattress. He ventured down the alley to look for the museum somewhere on the next street.

But he made it only halfway when a voice shouted out, "Freeze!"

19. Granglers Attack

"Don't ... move ... a muscle." The unseen voice was gruff—an earthling voice, male, adult.

Rolo was chilled with fear, afraid to turn around, afraid to flinch, afraid to even look. He had heard stories of street earthlings, wild strays roaming in hungry packs, desperate, vicious. His pulse pounded in his ears.

What Rolo did not see was even worse. Behind him, a pack of monstrous rogents, large stocky ones, each as heavy as an earthling, was crawling out of the sewer and creeping up the alley toward him. They were granglers, sightless predators with milky dead eyes, multiple rows of tiny spiky teeth, hardened claws, a patchy coat of dark fur, and a serrated ridge down their spine and tail. They usually hunted underground dwellers, but they weren't picky—any warm flesh would do. Their probing noses twitched, sensing live meat so close in front of them.

Rolo heard the rustling behind him. Slowly, he turned his head to peek.

Suddenly, with a hiss, the nearest grangler leaped up at Rolo, teeth out. But just as suddenly, it shrieked and fell to one side—with an arrow in its neck.

"Run!" barked the gruff voice.

Rolo ran. So did the grangler pack. He had seen only a glimpse of them, but that was enough, so he kept his head forward and fled from their hissing and the clamor of their claws scraping the pavement. He heard another shriek and a flop as an arrow struck down another one.

A figure flew past Rolo. It was the gruff man, swinging from a rope with one hand, holding a makeshift bow in his other. His hair and beard were long, messy, and streaked gray. His face was weathered and darkly tanned, with deep creases and thick eyebrows framing his steely eyes. His clothes were dirty and tattered. He was indeed a street earthling, a stray, a survivalist of the urban jungle. His name was Zeffro.

He swung onto a tall dumpster ahead and shot two more granglers. Then he grabbed a rod and banged a metal trash can repeatedly. The blind rogents squealed and bumped into walls, assaulted by the percussive din.

Zeffro leaped up to unhook another rope from the wall and swung down the alley. Spinning around with the rope between his thighs, he drew an arrow and struck down another grangler. He swung past Rolo onto another dumpster and tossed him the end of the rope. "Grab on, kid!"

Boosted by the adrenaline surging in his blood, Rolo scaled the side of the dumpster while Zeffro hoisted him to the top. Three granglers were right below him, clawing their way up a pallet and boxes stacked against the dumpster, while the rest of the pack surrounded them and hissed.

Zeffro yanked a rope dangling overhead, and a fire escape ladder slid down. "Climb!"

Rolo climbed. Zeffro stood guard, shooting more granglers with the last of his arrows, then he followed Rolo upward. "Faster!" he grunted.

They scrambled up the metal rungs, all the way up the side of the warehouse to the rooftop.

Rolo clambered onto the gravel roof and fell, panting.

Mysteriously, the gruff man did not appear. Rolo listened. There were still scratching and hissing sounds, but they were much quieter and distant. He waited, but where was the wild street earthling?

Slowly, Rolo tiptoed back to the ladder to look.

A little closer.

A little closer.

A grangler lurched onto the roof!

20. Zeffro the Stray

Rolo screamed and fell backward, scampering away from the foul, deadly grangler. But actually, he noticed, it didn't even move. It wasn't deadly; it was dead.

"Here, grab this!" grunted Zeffro from the ladder below, bearing the weight of the carcass and shoving it onto the roof. "Grab it!"

Rolo hesitated.

"Come on, kid! It can't bite you now."

Repulsed, Rolo warily grabbed the disgusting monster's front claw and pulled. Step by step, he slowly dragged the heavy carcass fully onto the gravel roof, then collapsed onto his back, panting.

Zeffro popped up from the ladder and peered back down into the alley. The grangler pack was retreating. "They won't be back." He grabbed the dead grangler's tail and dragged it effortlessly across the roof. "This way," he grunted.

Rolo followed Zeffro to a makeshift shelter—a roof of metal scraps propped up by two wooden sticks, leaning against the wall of a taller building. Within the shelter was a bar counter made of scrap wood, and upside-down buckets for stools. Along the back wall, crude shelves were stacked with various bags, bottles, boxes, and tools.

"Have a seat," said Zeffro while he hauled the carcass behind the counter.

Rolo sat on the bucket in the cool shade of the metal roof, catching his breath, still dazed from the shock of adrenaline. He gazed at the panoramic view from the rooftop. The cityscape sprawled in all directions under the serene yellow sky, and the scrappy bar somehow had an exotic charm. It felt surreal.

"You hungry?" grunted Zeffro.

"Sure!"

Zeffro reached down and heaved the monster carcass onto the bar, then raised an oversized cleaver overhead.

Rolo's gut clenched. "Oh! Ugh. What are you doing?!"

With a brutal chop, Zeffro decapitated the beast and butchered the carcass.

Rolo gagged and convulsed, hopping off his stool to look away.

Zeffro snickered. "Haven't you ever had grangler meat before?"

"Well, grangler *flavor* earthling chow."

"Where do you think that comes from?"

"I know, but ... I've never *seen* it before!" He tried facing the half-butchered carcass, but he winced and turned the other way—only to see the severed grangler head staring up at him with milky, dead eyes.

Zeffro carved two steaks and slapped them on the griddle behind the bar. This so-called griddle was actually a large blorxling clothes iron upside down, with extension cords running into one of the building's windows. The steaks writhed and sizzled as he pressed the blackish meat with a knife.

"Hey," said Rolo, "thanks for saving me down there."

"Sure." Zeffro pulled seasonings from the back shelves and crushed some leaves.

"I'm Rolo."

A long pause, as if he didn't hear, until he finally replied. "Zeffro." He placed a saucepan on the griddle, and mashed some berries and mixed in the leaves.

"You live up here?" Rolo asked.

"Yep." He sprinkled seasoning on the steaks.

"Like, *all* the time?"

Zeffro shot him a look from under his overgrown eyebrows.

"You don't have an owner?" asked Rolo.

"I did." He dragged the two steaks back to center as they tried crawling off the griddle.

"Don't you miss living inside?"

"Nope." He mixed some seeds into the sauce.

"Where do you sleep?"

Zeffro looked up at the sky. "Here. Under the stars."

"Doesn't it rain sometimes?"

"So?" He flipped the steaks.

Rolo looked back at the skyline to admire the view again. He noticed the museum building not far away.

The pause in the conversation made Rolo uneasy, so he filled it with more of his own talking.

"You know, I've never been this far from home before."

"No kiddin'."

"Actually, we're kinda lost."

Zeffro looked up. "Yeah, kid. I see that."

"I've never even been off-leash this long outside before."

Zeffro lifted the steaks onto two plates. He raised the pan and drizzled the thick red sauce on them. Then he sprinkled more spices and delicately garnished each dish with a small green sprig. With a cloth, he wiped sauce from the edges of the plates, and slid one in front of Rolo.

"Here."

Rolo's eyes widened and his mouth watered as he caught a whiff. "Wow, this smells amazing!" He looked around the counter. "Uhh, do you have any silverware?"

Zeffro stared at Rolo, grabbed his own steak with one hand, and bit off an excessive mouthful.

Rolo looked back down at the severed head, which now seemed to be sneering at him. He looked back at his blackish steak, which by now had stopped writhing. With just his fingertips, he gingerly lifted it to his mouth and took a tentative nibble. The tangy zing tickled his tongue and tingled his senses. The savory flavor was nothing at all like his tasteless canned goop or grangler-flavored kibble—and way better than any mushy table scraps that Zira slipped him.

"Oh! Oh!" Rolo exclaimed. "This is delicious! Mm!"

"It's fresh," Zeffro mumbled with chewed-up black meat spilling out of his mouth.

Rolo took a ravenous bite. Then another. And another. In a sense, Rolo was having his first taste of independence.

They continued to eat in silence as Rolo relished every mouthful, until reality so rudely interrupted his dining.

"Rolo!" called a distant voice through a broken skylight. It was Smuffins. "Rolo-rolo-rolooooo!"

"Oops!" said Rolo, suddenly remembering his mission. "I better take this to go."

Zeffro nodded, sucking the dark red sauce off his fingers.

"Coming, Smuffins!" yelled Rolo into the skylight. Then he shuffled back to the fire escape while tearing another bite from the steak in his hands. He turned again to Zeffro and gave a thumbs-up. "Mm!! Five stars!"

21. Blorzon Row

"Roloooo," Zira called into yet another alley. She was sinking into frustration, but clinging to hope. She worried so much about him. She thought he would be eager to come home, so why did he run away when he saw her? Was he mad at her? Why, what did she do? Or did Smuffins make him do it? Worries knotted in her stomach.

She and Riffa weaved their way along Blorzon Row, an old neighborhood shopping district with tiny stores squeezed side by side. Shoppers milled about the sidewalks in no hurry. Street vendors hawked their assorted wares, shiny trinkets, and eclectic antiques. Newsstands displayed racks of magazines, postcards, flowers, and candies. Small crowds lined up at food carts for hot tofustrami cones, bazooli root wraps, and mustrum-dough pretzels.

A street musician leaning against a brick wall strummed folksy riffs on a vibbertar. A shaggy blorxling standing on a soapbox preached gravely to no one that the universe was ending soon. Old neighborhood residents sipping targon tea outside a cafe argued about which clicketball team was going to win the next sport battle.

Riffa stopped at a clothing rack in front of a thrift store to look at a studded blurgenhide jacket.

"C'mon, Riffa," whined Zira, "we're supposed to be finding Rolo, not shopping!"

"I'm just looking." Riffa grabbed a blorange hoodie and held it up to her. "Hey, this color would look good on you."

"Really?"

"Yeah, you've been wearing that same ratty hoodie for like three years now."

"I thought you only shopped at Forever 147."

"What?" scoffed Riffa. "That was like two years ago. See, you don't know anything about me."

"Sure I do!"

"Okay, who's my favorite band?"

"Um. Blorgen Boyz?"

Riffa sneered at her. "Really?!"

Zira shrugged.

Riffa continued, "What's my favorite type of blizza?"

"Zepperoni!"

"No. That's *your* favorite. I like pineazzle—but Mom always gets us zepperoni. Do you even know what Rolo's favorite food is?"

Zira worried this might be a trick question. She thought she knew, but now she wasn't so sure. "Zirken tenders?"

"Nope."

"Yes it is." Now she was certain. Or so she told herself.

"Don't you ever notice how he just picks around it?"

Zira looked away and went silent. Why was Riffa picking on her? And why were they wasting time talking about this? They were supposed to be finding Rolo.

But Riffa persisted. "How are you supposed to keep any friends if you just ignore whatever anyone else likes?"

"I have friends!" Zira tensed up. She knew this questioning was leading to a dark place.

"Oh yeah? When's the last time Zailey came over?"

That was crossing a line! Her best friend Zailey had slowly grown distant and stopped accepting her invitations long ago. Zira never did find out why. It still stung.

"How about Lurna?" Riffa interrogated. "And Borza?"

Zira's face was flushing, simmering from embarrassment to shame, to resentment, to anger. "Why are you so mean?!" shouted Zira.

"Why are you so selfish?!" shouted Riffa.

"Why don't you two buy something?!" shouted the shopkeeper, shambling out from behind her counter in the thrift shop.

Zira looked down and avoided eye contact.

"Sorry," Riffa said to the shopkeeper. "We're going."

For the next few minutes, they plodded past the rest of the shops in tense silence. Zira felt wounded inside. She and Riffa bickered all the time, but this time it really hurt—perhaps because it was too close to the truth.

"I'm not selfish," she mumbled.

Riffa ignored her, which only made her feel worse.

They continued wandering through the maze of twisting neighborhoods of Old Blorgton. They had been searching for hours, but still they were no closer to finding Rolo, who didn't even want to be found.

22. Smuffins' Solution

"Smuffins, I'm here!" said Rolo, trotting back into the warehouse from his accidental adventure and fine dining.

"Yo dawg, where'd you go?! I was scared half to death they caught you!"

"No, no, I'm fine," said Rolo, taking a bite of the floppy, black remnant of steak in his hand. With dark red sauce all over his face and hands, he looked quite carnivorous.

"What the quasar you eatin'?"

Quiggles galloped up to Rolo, hopped on his shoulder, and licked his face clean.

"It's grangler meat," Rolo mumbled with a mouthful.

"That's what grangler looks like? Ich. Nnnope."

"Here, try it!" He held out the last floppy morsel. But after a quick sniff, Quiggles intercepted it with his grabby tongue and gulped it down.

"Sure, Quiggles, help yourself," Rolo sarcasticated with a smirk.

"Whatever," said Smuffins. "Let's get goin'."

Soon they were back outside, continuing their quest for the origin of earthlings, while Rolo recounted his tale of the vicious granglers and the heroic street earthling, much to Smuffins's horror.

Now, up ahead, they could see the museum on the next corner.

Quiggles skipped and swung around the lampposts, where they noticed one of Zira's holographic lost posters. But it was covered by another holographic poster with the Animal Control Force logo, Rolo's photo, and the text:

WANTED

Considered Unneutered and Dangerous!

Patrolling half a block behind them, an Animal Control Force tank hovered in their direction, sweeping its scanning beam side to side.

"Look out!" yelled Smuffins as he pulled Rolo into a doorway alcove. They flattened themselves against the wall.

From their hiding spot, Smuffins noticed a subway station further up the street. "This is too risky, dude. Look, there's a subway station. We can make a break for it and get back home!"

Rolo was dismayed. "Don't you want to find out where we came from?"

The Animal Control tank crept closer.

"Naw, I just wanna go home."

"And why is all our history missing?" persisted Rolo. "Isn't that suspicious?"

"Why does it matter?"

"What do you mean?"

The tank's scanning beam swept dangerously close to them.

Smuffins said, "It doesn't make any difference where we're from, right?"

"Well, maybe it does." Rolo felt confused, but determined. "I dunno ... it just feels ... important."

"How? How is it important?"

"Maybe ... maybe this is that something 'more' I'm looking for. Like this is what's missing. You know?"

Smuffins shook his head, but with a smile. "Naw, I don't understand. But that's okay. I still got yo back, dawg." And with a nod, he dashed out into the street.

He waved his arms at the tank and yelled, "Hey! Hey! Oh no, don't catch me!" Then he ran around the tank back in the opposite direction. The tank's lights strobed blorange and blorple, and its siren blared. It pivoted 180 to pursue the stray Smuffins.

Rolo looked on, stunned. Relieved and stunned.

The tank caught up with Smuffins. From its turret extended a long mechanical arm with a large hoop on the end. With a flash, energy strings formed a large net. Almost in striking distance, the net rose and extended further, until suddenly it sprang downward, trapping Smuffins in the glowing strings.

Smuffins yielded instantly. Within the tangled net, he turned around and saw Rolo and Quiggles running toward the museum. He smiled.

"Run, Rolo. Run."

23. Quiggles the Wild

Rolo was now alone on his adventure, with Quiggles as his only companion. But he was feeling more confident in this strange new city, and independence was feeling more natural.

Soon he reached the museum, a large, polished-stone edifice, rising up from the street corner with grand steps to the entry. The sign on the roof read, "Old Blorgton Museum of Science."

A scruffy blorxling street musician sat at the top of the steps in ragged clothes, playing a tarnished harmoxia. He had a burly pet tigeler resting on the ground beside him, with purple fur and white spots, wearing a studded collar and leash.

As Rolo and Quiggles climbed the steps, Quiggles made a silly face at the beast several times his own size.

The tigeler scowled.

Quiggles grunted.

The tigeler growled.

Then Quiggles squawk-roared and charged full tilt at the beast. Just as Quiggles was about to strike, the tigeler dropped its jaw open and let Quiggles trip into its mouth, then snapped its jaw shut.

"Quiggles!!" shrieked Rolo.

"Kiffy!" yelled the street musician. "Drop iiiit. Draaaawp iiiit!"

Reluctantly, after a long pouty look, the tigeler opened its mouth, but only a little—very, very slowly.

Quiggles's leg wiggled out. Then his other leg. Then his other leg. Then his arm. And other arm. His body and limbs flailed wildly, until his head finally squeezed out of the tigeler's mouth, and he plopped to the ground, covered in slobber.

Quiggles stomped away, wiping off the saliva. But gradually, he veered left and left, faster and faster, till he was now charging back to the beast. He snarled and leaped up onto its head, trying to bite its thick scalp.

The tigeler rolled its eyes.

"Quigglllllles!" Rolo scolded.

"Whoa there, little fella," said the street musician as he gently nudged Quiggles off.

"So sorry about that, sir," said Rolo, half embarrassed by Quiggles's wildness, but half impressed.

Quiggles gave a final growl at the tigeler, then strutted away with a smug sense of accomplishment, dusting off his hands.

Rolo chuckled. "Quiggles, I think you're my role model."

They now approached the museum entrance, finally arriving at the glassy gates to the secrets of Rolo's mysterious home planet. But a stocky security guard abruptly blocked their path.

"Stop there, earthie. Where do you think you're going? No strays allowed."

At the same time, Zira's voice yelled from a distance, "Rolo!"

He swiveled his head to see Zira and Riffa across the intersection, jogging toward him.

"Uh oh."

When he looked back, Quiggles was now behind the guard with his mouth stretched wide open, about to bite their leg.

"Quiggles, no!"

And then an idea flashed. He had a plan, and he would need Zira for this. He jumped up and down and waved his arms. "Zira! Zira!"

24. The Museum

Zira and Riffa jogged up the museum steps toward Rolo.

"There you are, you bad boy!" Zira said sweetly. "No more running away, okay Rolo Polo?"

Then he ran away. He skirted around the guard and yelled, "We're with them!" as he and Quiggles slipped inside.

That was step one of his plan: get into the museum.

"Roloooo," whined Zira. Riffa groaned loudly in agreement as they followed him inside.

The Old Blorgton Museum was shiny with buffed tile floors and polished stone pillars, gleaming with yellow sunbeams from the skylights above. A sparse crowd ambled about and perused the exhibits, while their voices reverberated in the vast space.

Once Rolo saw Zira was well inside, he turned around and jumped into her arms.

"Zira! You found me!"

"Rolo, you poor thing!" She hugged him tightly. "Were you scared?"

"Nope," he said with a smile.

"What's with you? Why are you acting so weird?" she asked in a sugary voice.

He chose to strategically ignore that question. Instead, he took Riffa's phone from his pocket and handed it to her.

"Here, Riffa."

"Finally!" she blurted, actually smiling for the first time all day.

Rolo wiggled out of Zira's arms. "Betcha can't catch me!" He ran into the exhibit hall. Zira fell for his trick and chased after him.

At the risk of repeating herself, Riffa groaned again.

With Quiggles riding piggyback, Rolo led Zira on a low-speed chase, zigzagging around the statues in the entry, up a spiral ramp, and across the elevated walkways in the tropical forest atrium. Zira was catching up—or more precisely, he was letting her catch up. He slid down the spiral trunk of a twisted helix tree, and Zira spiraled after him.

This was step two of his plan: get Zira to have fun in the museum.

He jumped into a replica of a primitive pedal-powered spiral-copter and lifted off. Zira hopped into an old pedal-powered flapping-wing plane and pursued. They soared, fluttered, and flopped across the exhibit hall and touched down near the dinovore displays.

Rolo and Quiggles climbed onto a tetraceratops skeleton. With a motorized whirring, they rode the mechanical monster around the exhibits. Zira climbed on an X-rex skeleton and engaged them in a game of dino-chase.

In the astronomy hall, they hopped on a large mobile of the Blorxian solar system. Each of them sat on a different planet—Blars, Blupiter, and Bluranus—spinning as fast as they could to see who could get the dizziest.

Meanwhile, the security cameras were watching. In the surveillance room, a guard sat in front of a wall of monitors, observing every corner of the museum. Behind him stood an elderly blorxling woman with curly gray hair, dressed professionally. She was also watching intently. She leaned over the console and zoomed in a camera on Rolo and Quiggles, who were running around and laughing. She zoomed in on Zira, chasing and giggling gleefully. She zoomed in on Riffa, sitting at the base of a statue, glum-faced, looking at her phone, scrolling, scrolling. The elder adjusted her eyeglasses with her antennae and leaned even closer to the monitor.

Step three of Rolo's plan was to get Zira to go with him looking for any information about the earthling planet. But they were having so much fun together, he forgot.

They waddled and giggled in front of the live pengrin exhibit. The pengrins imitated them back, stretching out their legs and walking like silly blorxlings, chortling.

At the blinsect exhibit, Rolo and Zira admired various shiny bleetles on pinboards. Quiggles followed behind, plucking each bleetle off the board with his grabby tongue. When Rolo and Zira finally noticed, they had to pry open his mouth and pull out each bug one by one, pinning them back on the boards—hopefully in the right spots, but not really.

In the medieval hall, Rolo climbed inside an old blorxling suit of armor. It was way too big for him, so he only fit in the torso, and Quiggles climbed into the helmet. Together they hobbled around and clumsily chased Zira as she whacked them with an antique sword, until they wobbled and toppled backward, spilling out of the armor.

They came across an enormous old catapult used to hurl boulders. Quiggles climbed up the catapult arm and into the bucket, while Zira and Rolo cranked the winch. Quiggles gave a thumbs-up signal, and Rolo grabbed the trigger release. But he froze when he looked up and saw a stern security guard frowning at him, with her arms crossed and one eyebrow raised. She hooked her finger, signaling them to follow her.

25. Grandam Zananna

The museum guard marched Zira, Riffa, Rolo, and Quiggles down a long hallway. She opened one of the office doors and led them inside. "Sit," she said flatly, gesturing to four armchairs facing a desk. They complied. The guard then left and shut the door.

The office walls were paneled in dark wood and mostly covered with tall shelves—filled half with books, half with assorted antique artifacts, and all a little dusty. Slits of sunlight passed through the blinds from two windows. The four wooden armchairs faced a large wooden desk, tidy and accessorized with the usual office supplies.

Zira glanced over at Riffa, who glared back at her with flared nostrils. Rolo looked ridiculously small in the oversized chair with his legs straight out, and Quiggles was just a tiny critter in his own enormous chair.

Tense silence.

Finally, the door opened, and the elderly blorxling woman walked in. She said nothing and took her seat at the desk. Her name plaque read, "Grandam Zananna, Museum Curator." Wrinkles of wisdom traced the features of her face, framed within her gray curls. She adjusted her eyeglasses

with her antennae and somberly studied Riffa's face, then Zira's, then Rolo's. Riffa's eyes shifted nervously under the scrutiny.

Zananna spoke slowly, softly, and deliberately, first to Riffa:

"Are you responsible for her?"

"No!" said Riffa defensively.

"Is she your sister?"

"Yes."

"Why are you angry?" Zananna asked patiently.

"I'm not!"

Zananna cocked her antennae. "You're not?"

Riffa tried to hold her tongue, but failed and blurted out, "She keeps getting us in trouble! She's such a child!"

Zananna nodded slowly, then turned to Zira. "How old are you, dear?"

"Seventy-eight," Zira answered quietly.

"Is that all? Why, you're almost my granddaughter's age." Zananna's expression was warming up. She focused back on Riffa. "Such a child? What is it you expect her to be?"

Riffa glowered for a moment, then mumbled, "I dunno."

Zananna paused. "I remember when *you* were a child, about the same age ... You don't remember me, do you, Riffa?"

Riffa's eyes widened. She was stunned.

"I was your fifth-grade relativity teacher."

"Ms. Zananna?"

"Yes, dear." Zananna smiled. "I recognized you instantly."

"I was a lot younger then."

"Yes. And much happier, too," Zananna said pointedly.

Riffa looked even more uncomfortable, but Zananna held her gaze.

Zira somehow felt surprised that Riffa was ever her age, as if big sisters were just born older.

Zananna glanced at Rolo and turned to Zira. "Is this your earthling?"

"Yes," Zira said quietly.

"Why isn't he on a leash?"

"Sorry. We lost it." She looked away.

"You lost it?"

"Well, we were in the park, and the earthling catchers were trying to take him and he ran away."

Zananna nodded. "I see." She leaned forward and said wryly in a hushed voice, "Those bots are just power-hungry. *They* should be put on leashes."

Zira looked up and smiled. She liked this mysterious old lady.

Riffa curled her antennae in confusion and asked, "Are we in trouble? Did they break anything?"

(Blorxian museums are not like those on your primitive planet. Here the signs say, "Please Touch," and blorxling kids are very rubbery and almost impossible to injure.)

"Oh, nothing is broken *out there*," Zananna answered, putting unusual emphasis on those last two words. She glanced at Zira and back at Riffa again. "I just suspect you two are a little ... lost. As long as nothing is *missing*, you're not in trouble." Again, she put unusual emphasis on a word. She turned to Zira. *"Is* anything missing?"

Zira looked back at her blankly, confused.

Quiggles shifted his eye left and right guiltily. Then he opened his mouth wide, pulled out a shiny bleetle, and placed it on his armrest—one of the dead bugs from the blinsect display.

Zananna looked at the bleetle, then at Quiggles, then smiled. She turned again to Zira. "What's your earthie's name?"

"Oh, this is—"

"Rolo," he interrupted.

Zananna looked pleasantly surprised. "Well, aren't you adorable, Rolo! You remind me of my dear Groogy, right over there."

She gestured with her antenna toward a large glass case on a table in the corner. Inside it was a teenage, earthling boy sitting on a large cushion, not moving, but stuffed to look alive. He did look somewhat like an older, chubbier version of Rolo, but his eyes were obviously glass, and they looked odd and creepy. Zananna continued, "He was such a pudgy ball of dreams, just like you."

Zira giggled and Rolo blushed.

Then Rolo said timidly, "Um, can I ask you ... Do you know what planet earthlings come from?"

"Your planet?" Zananna cocked her antennae curiously.

"Oh yeah," said Zira. "I tried looking online, but I couldn't find any information."

"No, of course not," Zananna said matter-of-factly. "That is because it was deleted."

"Deleted?" said Zira and Rolo together.

Zananna stood up from her desk and walked to the door. "Come with me."

26. Planet of the Earthlings

Rolo listened intently to Grandam Zananna, eager to learn anything he could about the mysterious planet of earthlings and why that information was missing. She led them through the back halls of the museum as she explained.

"It was the Big Delete of 7117. Planet Blorx had accumulated so much knowledge that we were running out of data storage in the nebula. This was quite a global crisis, and no one could agree on what to do. So one day, a renegade data clerk hacked into the core and simply deleted all the old useless information. Most of it was kat videos. But unfortunately, they lost all the earthling history too."

Rolo's hopes capsized and sank.

Zira asked, "Didn't anyone remember anything?"

"Nearly everyone had offloaded that sort of trivial knowledge to the nebula." Zananna pointed to her brain-chip. "So their memories were lost too."

They arrived at a small gallery in the back wing of the museum, where several ancient blorxian murals were on display. Some showed extinct creatures like shaggy marmoths and figures throwing spears. Some showed hieroglyphs around large pyramid structures. Some showed star constellations and planetary orbits. Zananna directed their attention to a mural of a large, blocky spacecraft shining beams of light to the ground, with humanoid figures floating up in the beams.

"But," she continued, "we do have clues in these relics. This mural here shows earthlings leaving their planet in an ancient spacecraft."

Rolo lit up with excitement. "Which planet is it?"

"The ancients named it ..." She paused dramatically. *"Planet Earth."*

"Earth?!" scoffed Rolo. "Like, earthlings from Earth?" That's not very creative, he thought, but at least it was easy to remember. "Where is it?"

"The scrolls say Earth is the third planet from a star named Sol, but they left no clues to where that was."

"What was it like? Earth?" Rolo's imagination was sprinting off-leash.

"We don't know," said Zananna. "The ancients never described it."

Zira asked, "So there's no other information?"

"Well," Zananna hesitated, "there is a little, but it's not very helpful. Let's see ..."

With great anticipation, Rolo watched her run her finger along one of the bookshelves, then stop at an old, thick volume.

"This is it." She pulled the book out, laid it on the table, and carefully turned the pages. "It's right ... here." She pointed to an entry and read. "Earth: mostly harmless."

Rolo peered at the book, but it was in an ancient language. "That's it?!"

"Yes, I'm afraid so, dear."

Rolo's hopes plummeted again. All he had learned was the name of his ancestral home planet, but nothing else. And it wasn't even a very good name.

"But," Zananna continued, "there are other stories that have been told about the fabled planet of the earthlings, passed from generation to generation among the old star explorers. They're not written in any book, so we don't have them here. But if anyone knows, that would be Captain Blarzenhook. You could probably find him at The Black Hole Tavern at the harbor. Tell him ... well ..." She paused in thought. "Just tell him Zananna sent you."

27. Unsettled

Riffa pointed ahead, down the road. "There's a subway station this way, near the boardwalk. That'll get us home."

They had left the museum and were now walking through a pleasant neighborhood. Brown brick row houses lined the streets, and trees with rich mauve foliage arched over the sidewalk.

Rolo rode on Zira's shoulders, tuckered out from a long day of adventure in Old Blorgton. He now knew where earthlings came from—a planet named Earth—so far away, so long ago. His quest was fulfilled, and he felt satisfied. Well, he felt like he *should* feel satisfied, but he didn't. He felt tired ... and excited. He felt relaxed ... and uneasy. He wanted to go home ... and he didn't. He felt ... unsettled.

The sun was now setting overhead, eclipsed by another world. The sky tinted from yellow to amber as planet Blorx and her sister planet Blorza floated across each other's orbits in a circadian waltz of day and night. The sun reflected off the arc of Blorza's horizon as they edged closer and closer, until they touched, like a kiss on the cheek.

This was Rolo's favorite time of day. He rested his chin on Zira's head and gazed into the

twilight sky, while his mind paced to and fro, stirring up old memories.

"Hey Zira? Why did you pick me?"

"What do you mean?"

"I mean when you first got me from the pet store."

"Oh yeah, you were just a little kid," said Zira. "What made you think of that?"

"I dunno. I've just been thinking about things. All I can remember my whole life is being with you. But I never thought to ask before. Why did you pick me?"

"Well, I always wanted to get my own pet earthie for as long as I could remember. I begged and begged Mom all the time for years, but she always said I was 'too young' to handle such a 'big responsibility'. But then Lazro finally talked her into it, so as a surprise they took me to the pet store. There was this pen thing with a whole bunch of little earthies, and you were in there. And you just looked up at me with this cute smile, and I knew you were the one: my little Rolo Polo."

Rolo's smile widened, and he hugged her a little tighter. His conflicted feelings now felt a little lighter.

Following behind them, however, an Animal Control Force tank was on patrol. Its scanning beam swept side to side, side to side, and soon it was so close that the beam swept across Riffa's back. Zira turned and saw the tank almost upon them.

"Hide!" she said hoarsely as she pushed Riffa off the sidewalk and through the bushes.

28. Lazro's Rocket

Zira and Riffa fell behind the bushes onto a small patch of purple grass, as Rolo tumbled off Zira's shoulders, and Quiggles followed.

"Why are we hiding?" asked Riffa, annoyed.

"Shh!" Zira whispered, "It's the earthling catchers!"

They all lay on the ground, peering through the bushes as the tank crept by.

Zira was filling with panic. They had spent all afternoon looking for Rolo. And since they finally found him, all she wanted to do was to get him home safe. But he was not safe yet, and she was so afraid that he, too, would be taken away from her.

The tank hovered past.

Then it stopped.

Then it reversed.

They held their breath and crouched lower.

The beam scanned back and forth, back and forth, back and forth.

Then, at last, the tank resumed forward, down the street, and into the distance.

Zira sighed with relief. "Okay, they didn't see us."

Riffa looked down and happened to notice something suspicious through the partly open zipper in Zira's backpack. "Wait a minute ..." she said in an accusing tone. She thrust her hand through the zipper and pulled out a shiny red and silver object. It was a small model rocket, toy-like, the size of her palm. Her temper ignited.

"Where did you get this?!"

Zira did not answer.

"Is this Lazro's rocket? Did you take this from the attic?!"

Zira sat up and clenched her jaw, defiantly silent.

"Zira, answer me! You can't take this. You're not allowed to touch Lazro's stuff!"

"Yes I am! He was my brother too!"

Her gut clenched from aching, and her face flushed with anguish. She glared at Riffa through watery eyes. "Give it to me!" She snatched the rocket from Riffa's hand.

"Zira, you're going to break it!"

"No I'm not!" She clutched it close to her chest.

"We need to save all of Lazro's things. You're being so selfish! Why do you even have it in your backpack?!"

Zira looked down at the small model and turned it slowly in her hands, over and over. Then she spoke quietly.

"I like to hold it. It reminds me of him ... He always used to take me with him stargazing, and we'd go crater sledding, and watch the rockets flying. He made this for his science fair project, and he let me help him with it. That was right before we lost him, that night he was taken."

"Well, he wouldn't have been taken if you didn't make him go with you that night!"

"It wasn't my fault, Riffa!" Zira fired back. She held her glare until Riffa finally backed down.

This is what Grandam Zananna had so perceptively sensed. This is what was broken between these two sisters. This is what they were missing—their big brother.

29. A Dark and Swampy Night

That summer night three years ago—after their slime battle in the Evil Queen's castle, and their zepperoni blizza dinner around the kitchen table—Zira, Riffa, and Lazro had settled in the family room to play a game of Bloogabugs. After losing a few rounds, Zira was restless to do something else.

"Hey, let's go ride our bikes at the swamp!"

"Oh yeah," said Lazro, "it's glowing now."

"No," said Riffa, "I don't wanna go out. And my bike's still broken. How about we play Blorgan Pong?"

But Zira persisted. "Well, *we* can still go, Lazro."

Riffa kept protesting, but in the end, Zira and Lazro left her behind. They climbed on their bikes and rode to the swamp, with Rolo riding in Zira's basket.

Glowing green gasses bubbled up from the mud in the sultry summer night, like a simmering stew. The neon haze rolled along the shore, casting an eerie glow across the filmy skin of the still water, while the long reeds nodded under the three waning moons. A colony of blorple-bellied flogs croaked a continuous cacophony, until they were suddenly silent.

Lazro came racing around the shore, with Zira trying to keep up.

"Not so fast," she yelled.

Their wheels slid and skidded across the muck, stirring up the gasses into bright swirling vortexes, and splattering each other with mud and laughter. Rolo clung onto the basket, howling and whooping at every swerve. Then Lazro skidded to a halt.

"Whoa, look at that!" he said in awe, pointing ahead. Past the knoll was a dark metallic saucer with lights flickering around its circumference, hovering perfectly still over the far shore. "I've never seen one this close!"

It was an alien spacecraft, the type used by the skinny gray aliens with oversized heads, which they called bobbeloids. These bobbeloids visited Blorx occasionally, but little was known about them. They were so reclusive that they usually flew away when spotted, and they never responded to any attempts to communicate. Despite the many recorded sightings each year, some blorxlings didn't even believe the bobbeloids were real, while others believed they actually built the Great Cones of Ziga.

Lazro was fascinated by bobbeloids. He had read many books about them and built a large collection of model saucers, which he proudly displayed on his bedroom shelves.

"C'mon," he said, "let's get a closer look!"

"No, Lazro," Zira whined, "what if they're scary?"

"Yeah!" agreed Rolo.

"Okay, then you stay here, and I'll take a quick look. Okay?"

Zira did not like this plan, not at all. "Please don't leave me, Lazro."

"It's okay," he said. "I'll be back real quick. I promise."

Then he turned away and rode off over the knoll and out of sight.

Zira and Rolo hid behind a thicket of swamp reeds, and waited. Minutes passed, and nothing happened. The saucer still hovered in place, unmoving. Eventually, the flogs started croaking again, crescendoing louder and louder.

Suddenly, with startling brightness, the saucer shot a wide beam of blue light downward, illuminating the swamp haze. The craft maneuvered swiftly side to side, sweeping haphazardly. Then it drifted directly toward them! Zira stifled a scream as she and Rolo ducked lower behind the reeds.

Then, as suddenly as it started, the glow went black.

There was silence. But just for a moment.

With a boom of thunder, the saucer zipped off in a streak of light, swallowed by the folds of clouds in the dark of night.

Zira trembled and squeezed Rolo against her chest for comfort, still hiding, still waiting for Lazro to return.

And waiting.

And waiting.

"What if he needs help?" she whispered. "Maybe he's hurt."

Rolo looked at her helplessly and said nothing.

"I think we need to go look for him," she said.

She put Rolo back in her basket and pedaled up the muddy path, retracing where Lazro had gone over the knoll.

"Lazro!" she called.

But no answer.

"Lazro!"

She kept calling his name as they both peered through the glowing mist, looking for any sign.

But they found no trace.

No footprints.

Only his bicycle, toppled on the mud, with the back wheel still spinning idly.

...

Zira and her family sobbed that night. There was nothing the authorities could do. And there was nothing the family could do. Just hope, and wait— hope he was alive, and wait for him to return. But a day passed. Then a week. Then a month. Then a year. And another. They kept his room ready for him, waiting. But even with the door closed, it was too much of a sorrowful reminder.

Eventually, against the protests of Zira and Riffa, their mom decided it would be best to pack up his belongings and store them in the attic, out of sight: his clothes and bedspread, his posters, his telescope, his books, trophies, and models— anything that was uniquely Lazro—all hidden.

Riffa never forgave Zira.

30. In Search of Blarzenhook

Rolo had quietly watched Zira and Riffa fighting, which was now a silent standoff. Zira still sat on the purple grass, slowly turning Lazro's rocket in her fingers. Riffa still sat with her head turned away, staring at nothing. He felt like he should say something.

"Um, I don't know if this is a good time to mention this, but I haven't snacked in like two hours."

Zira wiped her nose on her sleeve, and put the rocket back in her backpack. Somberly, they all stood up and pressed through the bushes, and continued their long journey home.

The sky ripened from amber to orange to a dusky magenta. The streetlamps flickered on, and the plasmic flies awoke for the night and whirred in aimless whorls of light. The sound of ocean waves was now audible as they made their way closer to the boardwalk, closer to the subway, and closer to home.

However, that did not mean Rolo was safe. Mounted on a lamppost overhead, a camera kept its vigilant eye on the neighborhood. When Rolo unknowingly stepped into view, it zoomed in and locked on him, tracking his movement.

But Rolo was not thinking about the earthling catchers anymore. His mind was still swirling about Earth. And then he saw a sign:

The Black Hole Tavern

That was the place Grandam Zananna mentioned! The sign had a large arrow pointing down a side road along the harbor. He felt a surge of hope. If he could find that Captain Blarzenhook, he might learn more about his ancient home planet. But Zira and Riffa were still in a sour mood. If he were to ask, he already knew what their answer would be.

He whispered to Quiggles, "When I give you a signal, can you distract them for me?"

Quiggles gave a thumbs up, then trotted ahead. Just as they were passing the sign, Rolo nodded to him and snuck off down the side road.

Quiggles acted out a mime in a box, pressing his hands against the invisible walls on all sides and twisting his face in exaggerated expressions. Zira and Riffa looked at him, perplexed. Then he pulled an invisible rope, losing a game of tug-of-war to an invisible opponent. Next, he held an imaginary umbrella and balanced precariously on an invisible high wire. Zira and Riffa turned to each other in utter confusion. That's when Zira noticed Rolo was no longer behind them. He was already halfway down the harbor road.

Zira ran after him, yelling, "Rolooo!" Quiggles crisscrossed in front of her feet in an attempt to impede her.

Rolo reached the tavern—a rustic clapboarded drinking hole overlooking the harbor. He could hear the muffled sounds of voices and glasses clinking from within. He looked up at the heavy wooden doors, which were more of a barricade than a portal for his small self. Zira was getting close. So he ran behind a nearby bench to use as a barrier between them. She caught up.

"Rolo, why do you keep running?!" she whined. "Be good. Don't you wanna go home?"

"Do you know what place this is?"

"No."

"This is where Zananna said we could find that captain, and he knows where Earth is!" Rolo flashed an eager smile.

"No, she said he *might* know."

"Well, I really wanna find out. Aren't you curious?"

Zira paused. "Kinda, but we need to get home."

"But what's the rush? We're already here. Can't we just go in and check? Please?" He put on his best sad face. He could see it was starting to work.

"Zira!" barked Riffa from up the road. "Come on! I wanna get home!"

Zira looked spitefully at Riffa, then turned to Rolo. "Fine! Let's go inside."

31. ACF Surveillance

The Animal Control Force Command Center buzzed with bots chattering intensely. Security video feeds filled the wall monitors, including the view of Rolo walking near the harbor. Text flashed in red: "Target Identified." Maps plotted Rolo's trail and positions of the nearby ACF bot forces.

"Colonel, we've got a location on the target, on Blocean Avenue heading north."

"Sir, the 2nd Platoon is delayed in sector C30."

"What's the hold-up?" yelled the colonel.

"Their wormhole transport slipped into a Möbius time loop, sir."

The colonel grumble-yelled, "Those cross-wired clunk-bots couldn't navigate their way out of a paper bag with a compass! Now where is that drone squadron?"

"They are airborne and en route, sir."

"Still? We're going to need more. Lieutenant, get a robo-sub out there in case they try to flee by water."

"Yes, sir."

The colonel squinted aggressively at Rolo's photo on the wall. "Okay, you mangy mutt. Your move!"

32. The Black Hole Tavern

Beside the narrow road lay the harbor, a maze of docks and gangways with rows of spaceships standing on floating launch pads. Each rocket was its own unique design, tall or taller, painted in distinctive colors, with its own personal character and purpose. The spaceships rolled on the tide, swaying leisurely in their own meter. A resting sealzling barked twice and rolled into the water.

Zira, Rolo, and Quiggles pushed their way through the heavy wooden doors of The Black Hole Tavern. Inside, astro-nautical decor adorned the dark-stained walls. Sconces glowed dimly, and plasmic candles flickered on each table overlooking the docks. The air was warm and thick with the smell of stale grog. Crowded along the bar, a haggard lot of blorxling star sailors chattered and clinked their drinks with equal parts cheer and wear. On a stool in the corner, an old stubbly-faced star-farer played a languid tune on a wheezy, worn squeezebox.

Rolo scanned the room wide-eyed. "How will we know which one is Captain Blarzenhook?"

Zira pointed at an old blorxling sitting alone at a table. "*He* looks like a captain."

Rolo was skeptical. "It can't be *that* obvious."

The old blorxling did indeed look like the blorxian archetype of a captain, with a captain's hat and a dark peacoat, and an eyepatch over his right eye. His face was weathered dull green, creased with woes, and layered with a grizzled beard. He held a large-bowled pipe in one hand,

while he sipped from a mug of green ale in his other. His one good eye squinted, as if trying to peer through a fog while lost adrift.

Rolo and Zira approached, disrupting his solitude.

"Sir?" asked Zira. "Are you Captain Blarzenhook?"

The old star sailor raised his eye to hers and sharpened his gaze. He lowered his mug, tilted his antennae forward, and scrutinized the both of them for a good moment. In a grumbly pirate accent, he finally spoke.

"If you be askin', I am."

Rolo was surprised it was that easy.

"Blarzenhook *do* be my name, but I haven't been called by that *rank* since my fated ship was torn asunder by the curs-ed kraken's tentacles coilin' out from under the Blorzian stratosphere. With death in its wake and wave, my hapless vessel's crush-ed corpse sunk into a gas-eous grave."

"Ooookaay," muttered Rolo, unsure how to react to such melodrama.

"Now how do the likes of you be knowin' my name, and where I dwell to imbibe my bitter ends?" He slowly tipped back a sip of ale.

Zira said, "Zananna from the museum told us you might be able to help us. Do you know her?"

Blarzenhook's eye widened, and he lowered his mug. He was always thirsty for a willing ear to hear his tales of misfortune. "Aye, I do ..." He stared off in thought. "And yet for all the world I wish I did not. Many a moons and tides and years have waned since sirens sang that name unto my ears. And now that you have spoken it, an ashen memory is relit—"

Rolo worried they were getting off track, and he was feeling bold. "Excuse me."

"—of a time my heart did beat in flame."

"Captain?"

"Yet now 'tis only ache that smolders from—"

"Sir!"

"—that name."

The old salt stopped prattling at last.

"Sir? Have you ever heard of the planet ... Earth?"

Blarzenhook raised an eyebrow and cocked his antenna. "Earth, eh?" Now with a captive audience, he sparked a plasma match and slowly lifted his pipe to his mouth, building dramatic suspense and setting the stage—only to be interrupted by a young, green sailor walking by, who slapped Blarzenhook on the shoulder.

"Oh no, don't get him blathering on about Earth again!" The sailor laughed mockingly, along with a few others in earshot, and continued walking past.

Blarzenhook grunted at the young sailor's back. He then restarted his dramatic tale.

"Earth, ya said." He raised the plasma match to ignite his pipe. His face glowed in the dancing blue light. Leaning back, he slowly exhaled a long, wafting swirl of fire sparks.

Rolo and Zira climbed onto two seats and leaned forward on the table. The old salt had not said anything of substance, and yet Rolo was already hooked.

33. The Ballad of Blarzenhook

Captain Blarzenhook reclined in his chair and spoke softly in a mesmerizing cadence.

"I've heard many a yarn—stories spun by salty star farers o'er generations of ages and eons of yore—legends of wayward worlds and beasts unbridled—chronicles of lore from every corner of the ever-capricious cosmos. Whether these dubious tales be true or not, I cannot affirm nor refute. So, with that bein' said, and with my ration of ale, just rest your weary feet, and you shall hear this tale told through the years—a tale of grave misfortune, a tale that ends in tears.

"It'was a voyage of fate for this humble green crew, a lively lot too soon to be lost. Aboard their shimmerin' ship they did embark afar, with hope to see the light of a giant reddish star, burnin' twice as bright. But the solar winds were flarin' up, and battered her hull with holes, and cracked her keel in two, tossin' them through the brackish blackness of space. Their fate had now come due.

"But fortune had a role to play, for by chance, they found themselves washed ashore on an island of green and blue, a world unknown in any blorxian lore. 'Tis true these castaways did live, but this new world was primitive and wild, with no way to call or sail back home. All hands were now exiled.

"On the morn of the new day in this strange new world, the natives came to welcome them with curiosity—these wee, docile bipeds, much like our domestic breed.

"But this hungerin' crew had rumblin' bellies, in need of tasty meat. These natives numbered so plentifully—such an easy catch to eat."

"Wait," Rolo blurted, "they *ate* them? They *ate* the earthlings?!"

Blarzenhook chuckled. "Aye, but not many, not for long—for their flesh had such a gamy taste, so gristly and tough to chew. So they turned their spears to the dinovoric beasts, and slaughtered and butchered them tooth to tail for lavish feasts.

"Now years begot centuries, and generations passed. The world turned white with snow and ice, and these descendants of Blorx kept fires blazin' for wintery warmth. Then by and by, to avoid cold demise, these diminutive natives crept ever so closer to warm up by their sides.

"And soon enough the castaways grew fonder more, and a bond did form among these companions of rapport. So they raised them and fed them, and protected them in flocks. They gave them tools and taught them crafts to cut stone into blocks.

"The natives were so grateful, so as tribute they created grand statues and great pyramids to honor the wise kindness of their guardians.

"Then one new moon, with a flash and a boom, a sky ship sailed the night with a wake of light floodin' out the dark. Three hundred cubits bow to stern, it'was the Blorxian Ark. It rained on them deliverance and tears of joyful mirth. So in pairs with all their human pets, they left the planet ... Earth."

Rolo was stunned silent, blinking, his mouth agape.

"Wow," uttered Zira, equally astonished.

Blarzenhook lifted his mug and tilted it back to slurp the last drops of ale. He wiped his mouth and sighed with satisfaction.

At last, Rolo spoke. "That was *not* the story I was expecting."

"Then careful what ya be wishin' for." Blarzenhook winked and lifted his pipe.

"Where is it, Earth?"

"Ho!" Blarzenhook raised his eyebrow and flexed his antennae. "You think it be real, do ya?" He drew a couple puffs from his pipe.

Rolo reflected on it and declared with determination, "I need to find out."

Blarzenhook nodded and exhaled a stream of fire sparks. They swirled in the air and settled into

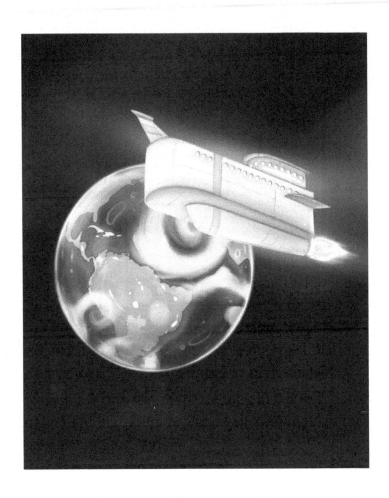

a formation of a star map. He took his pipe in hand and pointed the stem at a constellation that looked like a creature of sorts.

"They say the planet Earth roams about these here parts, orbitin' the last star of the constellation Kronarnious." He next pointed to a fist-shaped constellation. "Not far past the Cold Grip of Despair."

"What?!" exclaimed Rolo.

Blarzenhook chuckled. "It do be but a name, matey—born from the idle minds of souls lost adrift in the vast expanse of one's emptiness and meaningless existence ..." He waxed on for a good twenty minutes.

34. Home Planet

Rolo, Zira, and Quiggles strolled out of the tavern laughing. The night sky by now had darkened to a deep purple.

Waiting on the bench outside, Riffa looked up from her phone. "Finally! What took you so long?"

Rolo chuckled. "I thought he would never stop talking!"

"He was funny," said Zira. "I liked him!"

"Well, hurry up," Riffa grunted.

They resumed back along the harbor road, as Quiggles zigzagged about under the streetlamps, trying to catch plasmic flies with his tongue.

Riffa's brain-chip flashed while she looked up the subway schedule. "If we catch the next wormhole, we can make it home before 29 o'clock."

Rolo's smile dropped. Something didn't feel right. He stopped walking. The others didn't notice.

"Ooh!" said Zira to Riffa. "Can we stop for frozen quig-pops at the subway station? Remember we used to eat those after visiting the zoo?"

Zira turned and saw Rolo was far behind. "Rolo, c'mon."

Rolo sighed. "Zira, I ..." He had to tell her something, but he didn't know how.

She walked back to him. "What's the matter? Do you want me to carry you?"

"No. It's not that. I just ... I don't want to go home."

"What do you mean?"

Something about the word "home" struck Rolo. He thought of returning to his same old bed, the same old food, the same old toys, the same old routine. It felt so ... empty. He didn't fully understand till now what was really missing, what he really wanted. He looked up at Zira with empathy. He knew this would hurt her, and he didn't want to hurt her. But he had to. He took a deep breath and stammered:

"I want to go ... to go find Earth."

"Sure, and I wanna go to the ice cream planet." Zira laughed.

"Zira, I'm serious. I wanna go back to my home planet."

"Don't be silly, Rolo. *This* is your home planet, and that's just a story!"

"What if it's not? I think it's real." He tried to smile to win her over, but he didn't really feel like smiling, and it wasn't working.

"Rolo, you don't understand. You're just an earthling."

That stung: "just" an earthling. Zira was always dismissive of him. So were all the blorxlings, and they talked down to him and didn't take him seriously. He shot back, "I understand more than you think!"

"No, you don't! Now c'mon, let's go home!" Zira used her scolding voice now, which Rolo knew all too well.

"If you don't want to help me, fine! But I'm going to do this, with or without you!"

"Rolo, I said no! You've been running away from me all day, and I'm tired. Now be good and come along!"

Quietly, half to himself, he said, "No."

"Rolo, we have to go, *now!*" She reached out to grab his hand.

He stepped back to escape her reach. He felt his eyes stinging as he looked up at her. Heat rushed to his face. His ears felt muffled. A pressure built up inside him, until he couldn't contain it anymore. He erupted.

"You just don't understand me! You never even *tried* to understand me!"

He was shocked by his own words. He didn't like how that came out, but it was the truth, and he had to say it. He watched her stunned reaction, then he turned and stomped toward the harbor.

Zira chased after him, so he ran.

"Rolo!" she hollered.

Riffa yelled, "See? This is why you're supposed to keep his leash on!"

"Rolo!"

He reached the fence around the harbor, slipped between the metal bars, and kept running, followed by Quiggles.

Zira crashed into the fence and grabbed the bars. "Rolo! Come back here!"

He ignored her and fled onto the docks.

"Rolo!"

35. Moonlight on the Docks

Countless distant stars pierced the deep purple sky —homes to countless distant worlds. The three crescent green moons glimmered off the watery horizon. The two smaller moons orbited closely around the large moon, which sparkled with city lights and transport lines radiating outward in rings across its surface. A space tether climbed the sky to the moon, anchoring it to the planet, with twinkling transports crawling up to the lunar hub and back.

Rolo sat on a dock overlooking the harbor mouth. He dangled his bare feet into the water, feeling the slight charge tingling on his toes. The blorxian ocean glowed blue with every ripple and wave, like an underwater aurora, splashing brightly against the pylons and casting ripples of light. The tranquil sounds of the harbor were like a lullaby in the night—water lapping against the docks, boards creaking, a distant buoy clanging, and clickets and flogs chirping and croaking in rhythm. Rolo took a deep breath of the vinegary ocean air. He gazed up at an especially bright star and imagined it was Earth.

Quiggles, however, had no such existential crisis about where he belonged or the meaning of his life. He was in the water, floating on his back with glowing ripples, squirting water out his mouth like a fountain.

"There you are!" said Zira as she arrived at the dock, slightly out of breath, breaching Rolo's seclusion.

He did not look at her.

She approached and leaned down to pat him on the head.

He leaned away.

She paused, then sat next to him, but not too close.

"What's the matter, Rolo?" Her voice was quiet and shaky. "Why are you mad at me?"

Rolo sighed and tried to compose his words. "You just don't understand. I just ... I want to find something ... *more*. I want to go find Earth."

"But why? This is your home. This is your home, with me."

"I know, but—"

"Don't you like me anymore?" Her voice cracked.

Rolo was taken aback. "Of course I do! I love you, Zira. But something just feels ... missing. I feel like there's something more for me out there. I think I've been feeling it for a long time, but I really didn't know what it was until now."

"But why? You have me! And Quiggles and Riffa. Aren't we enough, Rolo? You're my pet. Isn't that enough?"

He could hear her deepening pain, and it pained him too. He reflected. "I thought it was. I mean, I love being your pet. But ... it's always the same thing, every day. I eat, and take naps, we play —"

"But you love playing—chase and belly rubs and flying into the beanbag."

"Actually ... no." He had always been afraid to tell her the truth, but now it was a relief to let it out. "I'm not a little kid anymore. I don't really like that."

"Yes you do," Zira insisted.

"I wanna make you happy, Zira, but sometimes ... it's just too much. It's suffocating."

"But what about today? That was different. That was fun, wasn't it?"

"Yeah, actually it was." He smiled. "It was a lot of fun. But still, I want more than ... fun. I want to, like, make something, or do something important. I dunno."

"Then I'll get you more toys! And we can get you another pet!"

"No—"

"But why! Why?!" Tears spilled down Zira's cheeks.

"Zira—"

"No!" Her tears quickly turned to anger. "You're my pet! You're mine! And we're going home!" She reached over to grab him.

"No!" He jumped up and stepped back. "Zira, if you love me, then please understand! This is important to me. I want to find Earth!"

"You can't go to Earth! It's ... it's not even real! And you couldn't even get there! Who would feed you? And keep you warm? And where would you sleep? You'd be lost, Rolo! Who would take care of you?"

"Maybe I don't need anyone to take care of me!"

"Yes you do! You're just a little earthie. *You need me!*"

His throat tightened. *"Maybe if you didn't take care of me, I could be more!* You never let me do my own thing, or try something my own way. Maybe I can do more, I want to, but I'll never know if you keep holding me back! Zira, please understand—"

"There's nothing to understand! You're my pet and we're going home. *Now!*" she commanded, pointing beside her feet.

He paused and took a ragged breath. "I'm sorry." He looked her in the eyes with sympathy, and guilt, and regret—but determination too. Then he turned and walked away.

Zira stomped. *"Roloooo!"*

Quiggles climbed out of the water and followed him down the dock.

As they left Zira behind, Rolo could hear her crying in the darkness, alone. It crushed his heart.

...

In the ocean water, a distance from the dock, a robotic periscope rose up. It rotated left. Then right. Then locked on Rolo and zoomed in.

36. ACF General Glirk

"Colonel, we located the target at the harbor!"

The wall monitors in the Animal Control Force Command Center displayed the submarine video feed of Rolo.

"Good!" yelled the colonel. "Sergeant, how long till ground troops intercept?"

"Sir, no ETA yet. Now their transport slipped into a time dilation drain-hole."

The colonel yell-grunted, "Those brainless bots would lose their heads if they weren't bolted on!"

He then pivoted to B-L1 and B-D3. "Privates, I can't believe I'm about to do this, but I'm sending you out to the field again. Can you two bolt-buckets manage to keep your nuts screwed on this time?!"

"Sir, yes, sir!" The two bots saluted and exited.

The colonel yelled quietly to himself, "I've got about as much confidence in those two as a plastic worm-gear! We're going to need backup." He pivoted and rolled up a platform and entered an office door.

"General Glirk, sir!"

Unlike the rest of the robo-tech command center, the general's office was just a regular office, old and outdated, with a scratched-up wooden desk, faded wall paneling, and dented filing cabinets. The back counter had stacks of holographic papers, a wilting potted plant, and a stained coffeine maker. A calendar was pinned to the wall, next to a poster of a kiffen hanging on a tree branch with the text, "Hang in There Kiffy."

General Glirk reclined in the office chair with her feet on the desk, reading a large holographic newspaper, with an empty coffeine mug to the side. She was a blorxling, not a robot, wearing an ill-fitting animal control uniform and cap. Unlike the obsessive bots, to her, this was merely a civil desk job, a promotion that no one else wanted, unimportant in the grand scheme of things.

She lowered her newspaper and sighed. "What is it now, Colonel?"

"General, we have an unlicensed earthling running feral in sector B41, considered unneutered and dangerous, abetted by two minors traveling north. The 2nd Platoon has been delayed. Requesting backups, sir!"

She shrugged. "Whatever."

"General, should we deploy the 1st Cavalry or the Special Strike Force?"

"For *one* earthling?"

"Yes, General."

She sighed again. "I don't care. Surprise me." She raised her newspaper and continued reading. The colonel continued staring at her, unmoving. She peered over the top at him.

"General, when should I surprise you?"

"What?" She rolled her eyes. "No. Never mind. Just ... do the first one, okay? And get out of my office!"

"Yes, General!"

"And close my door!"

The colonel pivoted 180 and exited—without closing the door. He rolled onto the platform and yelled louder than usual:

"Code Red! Sector B41. Code Red! This is not a drill!"

Alarms sounded, red lights flashed, and all the bots scrambled into frantic chaos.

37. Abandoned by All

Zira trudged out of the harbor gloomily. Out of spite, she had taken Rolo's shoes, which he had left behind on the dock. That way he can't get far, she thought. But she was already regretting it, so she set his shoes down by the gate where he might find them.

Up the road, she noticed a weathered, old rowboat on the dirt, grounded under the warm glow of a streetlamp. The wooden planks were cracked, the paint was peeling, and the bottom was rotting out. It looked as broken as she felt. She stepped inside, plopped down on the creaky seat, and set down her backpack. Delicately, she took out Lazro's rocket and turned it slowly with her fingers. The red and silver metal glistened under the lamplight.

With a heavy sigh, she lifted her gaze upward to the trio of moons in the deep purple sky. Lazro used to say that he was the big moon, Riffa was the medium one, and she was the little one, all in orbit around each other. But where was Lazro now?

The stars blurred in her tears.

Riffa saw Zira from where she was waiting on the bench by the tavern. She put away her phone and strolled over to her. "Where's Rolo?"

Zira took a ragged breath, wiped her wet cheeks with her sleeve, and locked her eyes back on the rocket. "He ran away ... to go find Earth. He left me."

"Oh." Riffa stood there awkwardly for a while before she stepped into the rowboat and sat on the other seat. She tried to sound cheery: "Well, we can get you another pet."

Zira looked up at her snidely. "You know you really suck at this!"

"Okay," Riffa said, unable to argue with that.

Zira looked back down and mumbled, "I'm *not* selfish, you know."

Riffa hesitated. "Sorry. I just meant ... never mind ... But why are you so clingy with Rolo?"

"What does it matter? He's my pet, not yours!"

"I know, but ... you hardly ever let him out of your sight. Why can't you just let him go?"

Zira's throat clenched, and she struggled to push the words out. "Because Lazro is gone. And Mom never talks to me. And you're always mopey, and you just ignore me ... Rolo is the only one who loves me." The tears burned in her eyes and spilled down her cheeks.

"*I* love you," Riffa protested.

"*No you don't!*" Zira shot back.

"Of course I do. I'm your sister!"

"*So?!* You're always mean to me! And you never wanna play or hang out with me. And you never lemme borrow your clothes or come in your room." She sniffled and looked back down at the rocket. "We used to be a family, you, me, and Lazro. We used to watch movies together under the blanket, and we'd put on costumes and make silly skits together, and we'd sing real loud in the car, and have splash fights in the swimming pool, and whack each other with pool noodles. ... But not anymore. And now Rolo left too, and I'm gonna be all alone!"

Zira crumbled inside. She bawled, trembled, and struggled to catch her breath.

Riffa's mouth fell open, but no words came out. She started to reach her arm out to comfort Zira, but she stopped short and retracted it back. Her eyes shifted uneasily, till her face flashed with an idea. "Hang on," she said as she got up and walked down the road toward a vending machine.

38. A Risky Impulse

After wandering aimlessly through the maze of docks, Rolo and Quiggles headed back out of the harbor. He had to find—well, he didn't know what exactly he was looking for, just some way to get to Earth. Still barefoot, when he reached the gate, he saw Zira had placed his shoes there for him. He felt a little relieved. Then he noticed Riffa across the road, so he hid behind a thin bush.

Riffa got two ice cream treats from the vending machine—zazzerberry sour squish, Zira's favorite. As she turned, she saw Rolo hiding, so she approached. "Rolo, I see you there."

He stepped out and said quietly, "Hey."

"You're not coming home with us?"

He shook his head.

Riffa paused. "She really loves you, you know."

He paused. "I know."

"Where are you going to stay tonight?"

He shrugged. "I dunno."

"How are you going to find Earth?"

This was the exact problem he was worrying about. He had no idea what he had gotten himself into, and he realized he had no plan. Perhaps he was too impulsive. He yearned to escape this dull, meaningless life as a pet, but he felt trapped, bound to this world with no way out. Overwhelmed and confused, he sighed and shook his head. "I dunno."

"Well, if you change your mind ..." She gestured toward Zira sitting in the rowboat, then turned and walked back to her.

Rolo didn't say anything. He stood motionlessly and watched Riffa leave, unsure of what to do next. He turned to Quiggles, who gestured back toward the tavern. Rolo took a long breath, then wearily, they walked under the streetlamps back to The Black Hole.

When they reached the heavy wooden doors, he hesitated. He looked upward, and there, dangling from the roof, he saw a wooden plaque with a curiously enigmatic inscription:

Behold the star you seek afar.
The farther you sail, the further you are.

...

Riffa rejoined Zira in the battered, broken rowboat, and handed her an ice cream treat. "Here."

Zira looked up and smiled a little.

Together they licked their cool, tart-sweet ice creams under the warm lamp glow, with a lone clicket chirping nearby. They were silent, but it was a healing silence.

"Do you have any more of those treats?" asked Rolo, who was now standing quietly behind Zira.

Zira lifted her head with a wide smile.

39. ACF Closing In

The bots chattered frantically. Video feeds on the wall monitors showed Rolo and his accomplices leaving the harbor. Large maps plotted all the ACF forces closing in from multiple directions.

"Sir, Privates B-L1 and B-D3 are approaching the target."

"Squadron 14 is about to intercept, sir."

"Sir, the 2nd Platoon has now fallen into a temporal cause-effect loop."

"Gah!" the colonel yelled.

"1st Cavalry is almost in position, sir."

"Sir, the targets are entering the boardwalk recreational district. High civilian density, sir."

The colonel yelled, "What are the weather conditions there? Get me a report ASAP!"

"Colonel, should we recall the robo-sub?"

Meanwhile, General Glirk had left her office with her coat over her arm. She trudged toward the elevators, pressed the button, and waited, watching the busy activity below. She never understood these nutty bots. The elevator dinged, and the doors opened.

"Okay, g'night everyone," she said with a lazy wave.

No one noticed her.

She stepped into the elevator, and the doors closed.

The sergeant read the weather report. "Sir, the weather is 'calm and balmy, perfect for an idyllic stroll on the beach with the sand between your toes in the ethereal moonlight,' sir!"

40. The Boardwalk

Rolo, Zira, and Riffa walked quietly along the road outside the boardwalk park. The night air carried the distant din of the roller-racer, bumper pods, and tilt-a-swirl—each with their own music playing over each other in a cacophony of melodies—and the bells, buzzers, and clanking of the carnival games.

Zira was finishing her ice cream while kicking a small stone ahead every few steps. Rolo carried Quiggles on his shoulders as they took turns licking his oversized ice cream.

He noticed a sticker on a lamppost: "Cut the Leash!" He looked up wistfully at the bright star, the one he imagined was Earth. He now felt foolish to think he could go there. Earth might not be real. Or it might be an awful place. And how would he even get there? Or find it? He had gotten his hopes up for nothing. And he didn't even know about Earth until today, so why was it suddenly so important?

"Rolo," asked Zira, "did you really mean what you said?"

"Huh?"

"About playing chase, and tossing you into the beanbag? You really don't like that?"

So she did hear him after all.

"No. It's kinda scary. And I don't like my belly rubbed."

"Sorry ... I'll try to be more gentle. I promise, okay?"

Rolo smiled. "Thanks."

This will be good. He was glad he finally talked to Zira and stood up for himself. He knew how much she loved him. And he had a good home, a great home. And he had Quiggles, and his friends. Maybe he was just a pet, but so what? Like Smuffins said, he should be happy with what he's got.

Riffa pointed ahead. "The subway is just over there, past the boardwalk, then we'll be home soon."

Home. It'll be nice to be home—off his tired feet, back in his familiar space, back in his comfy bed.

...

Zira chomped the last bit of her ice cream treat, still kicking her little stone forward as she walked ahead of Riffa. She looked fondly at the boardwalk.

"Hey Riffa, remember we used to come here every summer for Blormorial Day? And we had contests to see who could eat the most cornblogs?"

Riffa furrowed her eyebrows. "That's not the way *I* remember it."

"What do you mean?"

"I remember you eating too many cornblogs and candy and soda, and you got sick and threw up all over my white pants."

"Oh yeah!" she laughed. "And I remember you took me to the bathroom to puke it all out." She smiled to herself. "But you made me feel better." She tapped the stone further ahead.

"I did?" asked Riffa, surprised.

"Yeah. And it was a *lot* of puke."

"No, I mean ... did I really make you feel better?"

"Sure. You always did. You used to help me find my toys when I lost them, and fixed them for me when they broke. And you put bandages on my owies, and brushed my hair when it got all tangled —all those things Mom never did for me."

Zira no longer heard Riffa's footsteps behind her. Curious, she turned around and saw Riffa staring at her. She had an expression that Zira didn't understand, and her eyes were glossy. "What's the matter?"

"I forgot," said Riffa with profound emphasis. "I forgot all of that."

Zira didn't realize the weight of her words, or how much they impacted Riffa. But she did notice an old arcade at the boardwalk, The Fun Fusion Arcadium, glowing with waves of photons from all the games.

"Oh look, Riffa! Remember this place? It was always my favorite. And they still have that song machine! Can we go?"

Riffa half whined, "Zira, we're almost home. The subway is just past here."

"Pleeeease, Riffa?"

Riffa actually formed a smile. "Okay."

Zira sprang toward the arcade, skipping all the way.

Inside, it was filled with video games, an air slockey table, whac-a-nole, spee-ball, and a claw machine—all flashing colorful lights that lit up the otherwise dark space. Rows of prize toys hung on one wall. But most important to Zira was the song machine.

She punched in her song selection and picked up the mic. The music started playing the ballad intro, with the lyrics projected on the screen. Riffa, Rolo, and Quiggles caught up as she started singing:

> *Atomically the bond that we*
> *connect is no anomaly.*
> *Elementally, with empathy,*
> *it's the nucleus of family.*

As the drums kicked in with a peppy pulse, Zira felt Riffa's presence, now standing close beside her, singing with her in harmony. Zira's smile beamed so wide she could hardly articulate the words.

When I was stuck in the mud,
and I left it unresolved,
you helped me grow a spine,
'cause it was time to evolve.

When my patience exploded,
a Big Banging of frustration,
you helped me cool my temper
and find my constellation.

The matter is real,
but time's an illusion.
You help me think things back and forth
to start the right conclusion.

You lighten my load,
giving me such levity,
and raise up my hope
with your anti-gravi—

With a rackety crash, Privates B-L1 and B-D3 tumbled into the arcade, clumsily knocking over the whac-a-nole machine. They rolled straight for Rolo!

41. The ACF Attacks

Rolo jumped away from the two earthling catchers. He had come so far today and discovered so much, but foolishly they spent too much time away from home. And now the bots found him and would soon catch him and lock him up! If they could just make it home, he would be safe because, according to the precise rules of the Animal Control Force, pets only needed a license when they were not at home.

Quiggles leaped into action and slid across the air-slockey table. He grabbed toys from the prize wall and chucked them at the bots' foot wheels.

The rest escaped out of the arcade to the main boardwalk, but soon the clattering bots were in pursuit. They weaved through the crowd and around the concession stands. Quiggles caught up, and they ran through the fun-house maze of spatial distortions, which made Rolo queasy from all the stretching and compressing. They ran around the bumper pods, which caused the bots to spark and jitter on the positronic floor.

Rolo saw a carnival game with life-size stuffed earthling prizes, so he jumped behind the counter and hid among the plushies. The bots rolled by. His ruse had worked! He ran off in the other direction. But even in the noisy crowd, the bots sensed the pitter-patter of his little feet. They doubled back and pursued.

"This way!" yelled Zira as she led them to the Sky Lift ride, with chairs dangling from a moving cable stretched across the boardwalk. They all hopped in a chair as it lifted off, ascending over the heads of the two bots, who looked up at them in dismay, shaking their fists.

They made their great escape! Until they saw the bots hop in the next chair behind them.

The next ten minutes was a slow, uneventful "chase" as the bots' chair followed their chair at a constant crawling speed across the boardwalk. Rolo leaned forward on the safety bar, bored, dangling his feet over the edge. Quiggles had a prize bag of fireworks that he had taken from the arcade. He threw a firework at the bots just to make things more exciting. It burst in their faces, but they were unfazed.

Once the Sky Lift landed, they ran to an airboard rental stand. Riffa, Zira, and Quiggles each grabbed an airboard and took flight, balancing on the round saucers. Rolo rode with Zira, terrified as they soared high above the ground, spinning and swerving on the wobbly disk of death.

The two bots skidded to a halt, unable to reach the runaway Rolo. They turned to each other, and B-L1 said, "Release the Robo-Net!" B-D3 nodded and launched a large metal hoop from his torso, a rocket-propelled flying net made of energy strings. It thrust upward in aerial pursuit.

"Look out! Behind us!" yelled Rolo.

Zira engaged in evasive maneuvers, spinning and spiraling in nauseating loops. They flew through the flerris wheel, and the net followed. They dove under the roller-racer, and the net followed. They circled around the tilt-a-swirl, and the net followed. Quiggles flew nearby and threw fireworks and smoke bombs at the net, but it dodged and spun around the bursts.

They dove down toward the carnival games, weaving rapidly through the aisles as the net got closer and closer. They turned sharply left, right, right, left. The net followed their every move. Then Zira made one wrong turn, and the net swept across her board, scooped up Rolo, and carried him away!

"Rolo!" she screamed.

The net promptly returned to B-L1 and B-D3 to deliver their prisoner. The bots leaned in for a closer inspection. But Rolo seemed unusually soft. And fluffy.

"That's not the earthling!" yelled B-L1. "That's a plushy!"

The net looked embarrassed somehow, which was weird because it had no face. It spat out the plushy, arcing high over the beach, then it turned to pursue Rolo. But it was too late. They had already lost their target.

Rolo was now riding safely with Riffa; they had made a clever switch down in the carnival games. The subway station was a short way ahead, and Rolo felt relieved. It seemed safe now.

But then it wasn't.

From the dark sky above, the 14th Airborne Drone Squadron swarmed in, swirling around them, buzzing in their faces, and bumping their airboards. Rolo clung tightly to Riffa's legs as she and Zira swatted at the drones. Quiggles threw fireworks, taking out several pesky botlings, but not fast enough. So he leaped from his airboard and hopped from drone to drone mid-air, kicking and tearing them apart, and gnashing them in his teeth with a crazed growl.

Zira and Riffa dove toward the subway station while Rolo clung even tighter and squeezed his eyes closed. They crashed outside the entrance and ran inside, followed by Quiggles.

The surviving drones halted at the entrance, hovering outside with dangling wires, sparking and sputtering smoke.

Rolo and the rest pressed through the crowd of commuters. At the same time, General Glirk just happened to be leaving the subway on her way home. Rolo bumped into her and ran by. At first, she didn't recognize him, but then she looked again—he was the unlicensed runaway! She almost started to chase him, but then she remembered that she didn't care. So she shrugged and went home, leaving the petty job for the overzealous bots.

42. Almost Home

The earthling park was now blanketed in night. The moons glowed above, and the clickets chirped contently. Zira, Riffa, Rolo, and Quiggles exited the nearby subway station, relieved and tired. They were almost home.

Zira stopped to take in the tranquility. She pulled the model rocket out of her backpack and gazed at it tenderly, turning it in her fingers in the glimmering moonlight. It always gave her comfort when she was feeling lonely. But it was a haunting comfort, for it reminded her of losing Lazro as much as having him.

"Do you miss him?" she asked quietly.

Riffa looked back at her, then at the rocket in her hands. "I try not to think about it ... But yeah. I still miss him." Her voice cracked.

Zira reflected for a moment. With downcast eyes, she held out the rocket for Riffa. "Here ... I'm sorry I took it ... I didn't mean to be selfish."

Riffa gazed warmly at her, then gently closed Zira's fingers around the rocket. "No, you keep it."

Zira felt the warmth of her sister's hands on hers.

"Riffa?" Her voice dropped even quieter. "Is he ever coming back?"

Riffa stared into her eyes, hesitant to answer. "No ... he's not."

Those were the words that Zira expected to hear—the fear that she had always felt—and yet, somehow, it hurt more to hear them spoken aloud. They pierced a hole in her heart and passed all the way through, leaving a clean wound for the hurt to escape. All the suspense that had amassed over the years—the not knowing, the waiting—now began to spill out, slowly at first, then suddenly with a gush, a release of grief. Her eyes were bathed in tears, and she gasped in the night air, cooling the burning within her chest.

She lunged into Riffa and hugged her tightly, squeezing both arms around her back and pressing her face into her shoulder. Riffa felt rigid at first. And then she softened. Zira felt her sister's arms gently rest on her back, then felt her cheek rest on her head.

And then she felt Rolo's little arms wrap around her legs as he joined in the hug. And Quiggles's tiny arms around their shins. She and Riffa looked down and chuckled.

Rolo looked back up at them, smiling. But his smile slowly drooped as he saw past them.

"Um, I don't know if this is a good time to mention this, but we're not alone."

They followed Rolo's eyes and saw an enormous Animal Control Force bot behind the subway station, standing two stories tall, watching menacingly in the dark. Actually, five of them: the 1st Cavalry. It was an ambush!

43. ACF 1st Cavalry

With a startling mechanical clatter, the gigantic bots bolted forward on their spinning treads to surround Rolo, Zira, and Riffa. Rolo panicked as an ensign bot swung a wide hoop net down toward him. Zira rushed to protect him, but it was futile— the hoop came down around her too, trapping both of them in the glowing energy net.

Riffa lunged for the net and tried to pry it off the ground. "Let them go! You can't do this!" she yelled. But the massive hoop was immovable.

Quiggles hurled his last firework at the bot. It struck its face with a ding, then fell to the ground and sputtered pathetic sparks and wispy smoke. The bots were unimpressed.

A petty officer bot slid open the reinforced hatch doors in its towering torso, a containment cell to hold the wild, feral Rolo.

In the nearby treetops, several squirlers watched the spectacle with glee, pointing at Rolo with their little paws, and cackling manically with little squeaks.

Meanwhile, Smuffins and Yoola were home sitting on their front porch overlooking the earthling park. Yoola noticed the five colossal bots in the distance, but that's all she saw.

"Oh look," she said, "it's your buddies the earthling catchers! Better not run away again." She smiled mockingly and pointed to the blinking tracking device strapped around Smuffins's neck.

"Ha ha," he sarcasticated.

Then Yoola noticed something else. "Look, that's Rolo! We need to help him!"

Smuffins instantly devised a solution. He said in all seriousness, "Let's get ... *the toys!*"

Yoola grabbed her bazooka-shaped automatic ball launcher. She cocked it, and the air squeaked as the chamber pressurized.

Smuffins powered up his hover drone with an ominous hum. He put on the piloting helmet with a heads-up display. The drone elevated, and its eight red laser pointers converged on a single focal point.

Meanwhile, Rolo tried to claw his way through the net as it scooped him and Zira off the ground.

Smuffins and Yoola ran toward the park with toys in hand. As they passed by Fabli's house, they saw him in the window.

"Fabli," hollered Yoola, "come help. We need to save Rolo!"

"But my competition is tomorrow!" yelled Fabli.

Rolo attempted to climb out the top of the net, but it was too high off the ground. The massive bot pivoted, swinging them in the net toward the petty officer's containment cell. Zira screamed.

Quiggles tipped over a nearby garbage can, spilling the contents and throwing them at the bots one at a time—paper cups, soda cans, water bottles, a chewed-up blizbee, and a bag of fast food scraps.

The net extended forward, slowly enclosing Rolo and Zira in the containment cell.

Suddenly, a drone flew around the bots' heads, aiming red lasers at their optical sensors. Smuffins stood nearby, piloting the drone and shouting to them, "Now let's see if *you* can catch the red dot!"

A laser dot landed on the commander bot's face. Another ensign took action and swatted its massive grappler at the elusive spec, slapping the commander with a clang. The commander slowly swiveled its head and looked at the ensign derisively. The ensign looked away innocently, suddenly taking great interest in the beautiful stars above.

Yoola charged in with her automatic ball launcher and fired trennis balls at their heads, aiming for their ear holes. With each shot, she yelled, "Fetch *this!* Fetch! Fetch! Fetch!"

Even the squirlers joined the fray. They weren't on anyone's side; as rogents of chaos, they simply liked to stir up mayhem. With cheek-fulls of acorns, they scrambled up the giant bots' bodies and slipped inside through their cracks and crevices, tickling them.

The bots were fazed and frazzled. They swiveled and wobbled, knocking into each other, and dropped the net. Rolo and Zira scrambled out of the containment cell and down the net handle, then ran between the bots' legs and escaped into the park, along with Riffa and Quiggles.

The bots rolled out to pursue, but they were too dizzy and disoriented, leaning and listing left and right. They cocked their heads sideways and hopped up and down to shake the trennis balls and acorns out of their ears. The squirlers cheered from within.

Rolo, Zira, Riffa, and Quiggles raced across the field toward home, joined by Smuffins and Yoola. But now that the bots had cleared their heads, they were closing in too quickly.

At that moment, Fabli hurdled over the fence and dashed in front of the bots, knifing his arms through the air like a speed-runner.

"Split up!" he yelled.

They did, each running in a separate direction. The bots focused their pursuit only on the four earthlings, but they couldn't tell them apart, so they split up to catch them all.

Two bots chased Fabli as he ran to the obstacle course. He scrambled through the tunnel, jumped through the hoop, and ran up and down the ramps. He got so focused on the agility course that he ran back through the poles, weaving side to side, then leaped over the high jump bar, now racing directly toward the bots.

The bots stared at him and cocked their heads.

"Fabli, focus!" yelled Yoola as she ran by.

He looked up at the bots—"Oh yeah"—then ran off.

The massive machines pivoted and spun their treads to chase Fabli, splashing mud and grass on him.

"My hair!" he squealed.

Rolo and Quiggles rejoined Riffa and Zira. They had a clear path home now. While four of the bots were busy chasing the wrong earthlings, one was gaining on them quickly.

"We can make it!" yelled Zira.

Riffa looked over her shoulder. "No, they're too close. This way!" She turned and led them toward a different corner of the park.

By now, the other bots realized Yoola, Smuffins, and Fabli were not the fugitive earthling, so they rolled into formation in pursuit of Rolo.

"Where are we going?!" Zira yelled.

Rolo was confused too. Why weren't they going home?

"You'll see," said Riffa.

She picked up Rolo and hopped over the earthling-sized fence, and Zira and Quiggles followed. Undeterred, the five giant bots plowed through the fence, shredding it into metal scraps.

Riffa led the others into the woods outside the park, passing between the tall trunks, beneath the dark canopy of leaves.

The colossal bots skidded to a halt. The trees were too dense for them to pass.

"Commander, what do we do now?" asked the petty officer in a deep voice.

The commander swiveled its head in disbelief. In a deeper voice, it said, "We wait."

They stood guard at the edge of the woods, looking quite stoic and intimidating. Until they all started squirming. From deep within their metal bowels echoed squeaky, maniacal laughs from the cheeky squirlers.

...

Back in the Command Center, Colonel C-4 watched every moment of the chase on the large wall monitors. Realizing defeat, he growled and smashed his fist down on the console. *"Scrap metal!"*

But then the gears in his head started turning. The colonel was optimized for the Animal

Control Force—he lived for the conquest and the thrill of the chase. And today was the most exhilarating battle he had fought since his glory days in the robot wars. Most earthlings didn't put up much of a fight, and they were easy to catch—too easy. But Rolo and his crafty crew of rebel allies proved to be a most worthy adversary, and the colonel was genuinely impressed. His mouth twisted upward into something resembling a smile, and he chuckled.

"You magnificent mongrel," he yelled quietly to himself.

44. In the Woods

Zira and the others stood in the dark woods, panting and watching the five towering bots. With menacing, glowing eyes, the bots paced just outside the trees, sweeping spotlights across the tree trunks. They were in a standoff: the bots could not enter the woods, and Rolo could not leave.

"See, they can't get us here," said Riffa.

"Okay," said Rolo, "but what are we going to do? They're just going to wait there and catch me when we finally go home."

Zira wondered that too. How were they going to get home?

"About that ..." said Riffa. She sat on a nearby log and patted the space next to her. "Zira ... here, sit down."

Zira looked at her curiously and sat beside her. "What?"

"Zira ..." She took a deep breath. "Every day and every year since those aliens took Lazro, we hoped he was still alive, and we wished they would let him come back to us ... home. Well, that's what Rolo wants too, to go home."

"We *are* going home."

"Not *our* home ... *his* home."

"Oh." And then the realization sank in deeper. "Ohhh ..."

"Do you understand?"

Zira's thoughts and feelings turned against each other as she started to question things she had not questioned before.

Riffa continued, "Maybe it's time to let go, you know? Time to move on ... All of us."

Her words were heavy. Zira thought about Lazro, and imagined what it must have been like for him to be trapped in a world that wasn't his own, wanting to come home. She thought about Rolo, and what he kept trying to tell her—what she didn't want to hear, what she wasn't ready to hear.

"Zira?" asked Riffa delicately.

Zira sniffled and wiped her nose. Then, with a newfound determination, she stood.

"Okay, I know what to do ... Follow me."

Zira led the others up a winding trail through the dense woods, which gradually turned uphill, climbing higher and higher.

The sky was blacked out by the thick canopy of foliage, but the trees provided their own illumination. Glowing seeds dropped from the treetops—helicopter seeds that spun in their descent, tracing luminous spirals in the air, sprinkling sporadically among the sprawling roots. A nightinowl cooed a mournful sonata while the

clickets chirped in pizzicato, accompanying the aerial ballet of lights.

"I don't understand," said Rolo, trailing behind her. "What do you mean, *my* home?"

"You'll see," said Zira.

"Wait, tell me now. I wanna know."

She stopped and smiled at him. "I know how you can go find Earth."

"Earth? Really? How?"

She smiled more. "You'll see."

45. Rolo's Wish

After hiking through the dark woods, Zira, Rolo, Riffa, and Quiggles summited at a flat clearing overlooking the rolling landscape. They could now see the stars again, so numerous they looked more like radiant mist than individual specks. The three sibling moons beamed brightly upon the stony plateau.

Zira was satisfied. This was the right place. She set down her backpack and pulled out Lazro's rocket. She looked at it tenderly one last time, and gave it a sentimental kiss.

"Here." She handed it to Rolo. "I want you to have this. You can take this to find Earth."

Rolo looked at the toy rocket in his hand, puzzled and perplexed. He turned to Riffa. "Did she get enough snacks to eat?"

"No, silly," laughed Zira. "It gets bigger. Just soak it in water."

"Oh." He looked around. "But we don't have any water."

Then Quiggles strutted by, snatched the rocket from Rolo's hand, and tossed it into his surprisingly large mouth.

"Quiggles, no!"

Quiggles hummed leisurely while swishing the rocket around his mouth. He spat it out and placed it on the ground. They stared at it in anticipation.

Then, sure enough, the shiny red and silver rocket started to swell, expanding unevenly, almost like it was inflating. The bottom grew fat, then its stubby fins grew to size. It leaned left, then right, as it grew taller and taller. Until finally, it stood solidly upright, full-sized.

But Rolo still looked confused. The rocket was not much taller than he was. "Uh. I still don't see how this helps."

Zira smiled. "Look inside."

The round hatch twisted open.

Rolo stepped up to the rocket and leaned inside. "Whoa!" His voice echoed. "It's huge in here! Is that a flooshball table? And a hot tub?!"

Zira giggled. "Yeah. Lazro let me help him make it for his science project. Everything works."

On one fin was the name "Pea-Pod" painted in Lazro's handwriting—his nickname for Zira.

Rolo could barely get any words out. "Zira, I don't ... I ... Really?"

She nodded. "It's got everything you'll need."

"Wow. I ... I mean, of course I want to find Earth. But I can't leave you. This is the only home

I've ever known. You raised me, and ... I don't think I can do this."

"Yes you can, Rolo Polo." She kneeled in front of him and put her hands on his shoulders. Tears welled in her eyes. "You're the bestest pet ever, Rolo. You were always there for me, as long as I can remember. You played with me, and you stayed with me when I was sick, and when it was stormy and I was afraid of the thunder, and when I was lonely ... But you're more than just my pet. You should have your own life now."

His eyes glistened, and he beamed a bittersweet smile. "Thank you," he mouthed, but he was so choked up only a squeak came out. He flung his arms around her and hugged her with all his heart.

Zira loved Rolo's hugs. Warm memories filled her. Memories of their first hug, when she saw him in the pet store, just a little boy with a big smile, and he reached out to her and nestled under her chin. Memories of when he fell asleep on the sofa, and she would pick him up to take him to bed, and he wrapped his arms around her neck and laid his head on her shoulder. Memories of when she came home from school and stepped off the school bus, and he would run up the sidewalk and leap into her arms. Memories of when she took him for rides on her bike, and he hung onto her shoulders and begged her to go faster, and squealed with joy, and hugged her tightly. And memories of that night when Lazro was taken, and she was curled up in bed, sobbing, and Rolo climbed up and leaned on her and hugged her with his whole body.

And now this would be their last hug ... ever.

She held his hands and looked into his smiling eyes, their cheeks wet with tears.

He asked, concerned, "Are you going to be alright?"

She looked up at Riffa, who gave her a little smile. She knew she would not be alone anymore. "Yeah, I'll be okay." She squeezed his hands, then let him go.

Quiggles strutted up to the rocket and hopped in. He found a captain's hat inside and put it on—a perfect fit.

Rolo took his ID tag off his neck and placed it in Zira's hand. "I guess I won't be needing this anymore."

She smiled and gripped it tightly. A new memento to keep her company.

Rolo stepped up to the rocket, climbed the ladder, and crawled inside. He looked back at them gratefully through the hatch. "Thank you, too, Riffa. Take good care of her, okay?"

Riffa smiled and nodded. Then, with a sudden realization, she turned to Zira. "What are we going to tell Mom?"

Rolo gave his wry smile. "Just tell her I went to a nice farm upstate, where I could run around and chase squirlers."

A laugh escaped from both Zira and Riffa.

"Be good," he said to Zira, waving goodbye as the hatch slowly twisted shut.

Zira leaned back against Riffa's shoulder and felt her warmth. The engine ignited with a burst of brightness, then slowly, effortlessly, the rocket elevated off the ground and above the trees, blowing the glowing seeds into swirling whorls of light. Riffa wrapped her arm snugly around Zira, while Zira placed her hand over Riffa's and held it tightly. Through watery eyes, Zira watched the shining light rise higher and higher into the night, until it faded away among the stars.

Rolo was on his way home now, to the home he never knew—Earth.

Epilogue

Perhaps your cute, little earthling mind is too restless to let the story end there. So, I shall explain what happened next.

That night, scampering about the woods, a few squirlers took a moment to shed a tear for Rolo. Even though he was their nemesis, he was one of their favorites.

Smuffins and Yoola were sad to learn that Rolo had left. They never even got to say goodbye. But they understood, and they were proud of their friend, especially Smuffins. In fact, they even felt a little inspired. They decided maybe there were higher goals in life than just car rides, so they taught themselves to build their own pet toys.

Despite the muddy hair disaster the night before, Fabli won Best in Show at the Blorxminster Kennel Club. After that, he was too famous to visit the regular park anymore. *Earthling Fancy* magazine featured his photo on the Blebruary cover, and he was selected as the spokespet for Blurtho brand grangler-flavored earthling chow.

The earthling rights activists from BETA (Blorxlings for Ethical Treatment of Animals) got a law passed requiring earthling toilets to be installed in the park to replace the communal litter box. But most earthlings didn't understand how to flush the fission-vortex toilets, so they counter-protested to bring back litter boxes.

The Animal Control Force nearly caused half the planet to get sucked into a black hole while trying to trap a runaway shlamster. Due to that slight mishap, the blorxian government reassigned all the robots to the newly formed Garbage Collection Force. From then on, the cities were spotless! However, the bots threw thousands of blorxlings in jail for littering violations and for putting recycling in the wrong bins. General Glirk retired from the force and finally started her lifelong passion project: knitting homemade costumes for earthlings.

Zeffro expanded his scrappy shelter into a rooftop bistro, attracting crowds of stray earthlings for delicious dining overlooking the twinkling cityscape. His house specialty was, of course, alley-fresh grilled grangler steak with burgunbleaux sauce. However, his customers did insist that he provide silverware.

Captain Blarzenhook started volunteering at the Old Blorgton Library on weekends to regale children with tales of adventure from his space-faring days, whether they were true or not. The little green blorxlingettes squealed in fear and hid their faces whenever he got to the scary parts, but they always came back for more. Occasionally, Grandam Zananna stopped by to listen, which put a twinkle in Blarzenhook's one good eye.

...

When Zira and Riffa's mom returned home at the end of the week, she was shocked to hear about the girls' adventure. At first, she was very upset that they went all the way across the planet without permission and stayed out so late on a school night. But she was also proud and impressed by how independent and responsible her daughters were becoming (although not fully honest, for they did not tell her about giving away Lazro's rocket, which she did not notice). She could not comprehend why Rolo wanted to run away from home, and frankly, she gave up trying to make sense of it. She asked Zira if she wanted another earthling.

Zira thought about it, then with a flash of excitement, she asked, "Can I get a plony?"

"Are you kidding me, young lady? Those are even worse than earthlings!"

So Zira decided she'd just get a blabbit for now.

Zira and Riffa continued to bond. Riffa regularly played Blorgan Pong with her and defeated her every time. But for Zira, that was not the point. Over time, Zira's old friend Zailey even started visiting again and joined them. They all had splash fights in the pool, and went crater sledding, and baked cookies together. (Although Zira usually ate half the cookie dough when Riffa wasn't looking ... then she had to puke it out.) One day Riffa let Zira practice putting makeup on her. Zira intentionally did a bad job just to see Riffa's reaction when she looked in the mirror. After that, it was an ongoing war of hilarious pranks and counter-pranks.

Riffa still called Zira "Squid Squirt," but now it was an endearment delivered with a smile.

...

Rolo and Quiggles embarked on their unlikely road trip with no map, only a legend and a destination. They started at the hyperway onramp for I405 to North Polaris, then T70 to New Sirius, then DS9 to Las Vega. Quiggles did all the driving, which was a relief for Rolo since he couldn't grasp the concept of the stick-shift quantum paradox drive.

They often stopped to grab space food at drive-thrus, even though the grangler burgers never tasted as good as Zeffro's cooking. To pass the time on long hyperways, they played flooshball, but Quiggles always won because he played with both hands and all three feet, which was not fair. When they saw a billboard for "Galaxy's Largest Ball of Superstring, 12 parsecs," they made it their secondary mission to stop at every tourist trap along the way to acquire an impressive collection of kitschy souvenirs. At one point, they were delayed when a giant green hand grabbed their rocket—apparently, the Cold Grip of Despair was not completely made up.

Several months into their journey, while following a tip from an old Gudjan fortune teller they met at a carnival, they got a flat fusion reactor in the middle of nowhere. When they pulled off the hyperway to get the spare from the trunk, they were stunned by what they saw. With Rolo in the captain's chair and Quiggles at the helm, they stared at the viewscreen for minutes, astonished, their mouths agape. Then Rolo slowly leaned over the armrest and spoke into the mic:

"Mission Log, Commander Rolo, Day 157. I think … I think we found it!"

Before them, shining brightly in the black of space, was a beautiful deep blue planet, with great patches of green, and streaks and swirls of white. It looked so calm, so delicate, and welcoming. It was, indeed, Earth.

They were uncertain of what to do next or what to expect.

Then, over the radio, they heard a crackle.

And then a voice. A human voice.

"Unidentified vessel, this is Earth Base 42. Do you copy?"

Rolo looked at Quiggles in disbelief. His palms were sweaty. His stomach quivered.

"Unidentified vessel, what is your destination?"

Rolo nervously leaned closer to the mic, pressed the button, and spoke in a shaky voice.

"Earth Base 42. This is Rolo. My destination is ... here ... home."

To be continued...

No earthlings were harmed during the making of this textual record.